This edition published in 1995.

Written by Anne McKie. Illustrated by Ken McKie.

Published by
Grandreams Limited
Jadwin House, 205/211 Kentish Town Road, London, NW5 2JU.

Printed in Czech Republic.

My Greatest Book Of
BEDTiME STORiES

Starry Night Stories

When day is done and the sun sinks to rest, that's the time everyone should be thinking of going to bed.

When shadows of evening draw across the sky and the moon drifts over the trees, that's the time for bedtime stories.

Stories to tell again and again of soft brown bears, tiny mice and things that swim and fly. Stories of snowmen that dance in the dark and toys that come alive for just one night.

Tales before bedtime we all love to hear, they make us want to stay and listen...Just one more, please!

Contents

The Little Lost Hedgehog

Mrs Hedgehog had such a large family that she had to wash lots of clothes everyday.

When the weather was warm and breezy, all ten young hedgehogs lent a hand, and the washing was done in next to no time.

"Today is perfect for washing our clothes," said Mrs Hedgehog, as she gave everyone a job. "Two of you scrub the clothes, two of you rinse off the soap suds, two of you wring them dry, two of you hang them on the line, and two tiny ones hand me the pegs!"

Very soon all the dirty clothes were clean and bright and hanging on the clothesline in the sun.

"We all deserve a rest," smiled Mrs Hedgehog. So she sat down on the grassy bank near the clothesline, took off her hat and put it down by her side. All her little hedgehogs sat beside her with glasses of cool lemonade and buttery biscuits.

"How lucky I am," thought Mrs Hedgehog, "to have such helpful children." All of a sudden she gave a

squeal. "There are only nine of you! Where is Baby Hedgehog?"

The young hedgehogs put down their lemonade and biscuits and began to search at once. They looked everywhere, in the house, in the garden, in the meadow, in the wood, they even looked in the empty clothes baskets.

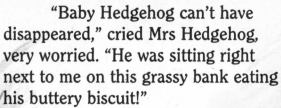

"Baby Hedgehog can't have disappeared," cried Mrs Hedgehog, very worried. "He was sitting right next to me on this grassy bank eating his buttery biscuit!"

The rest of that day all the hedgehogs searched long and hard. The sun began to set behind the hill and soon it would be dark.

"We must have searched everywhere," sighed Mrs Hedgehog as she wiped a tear from her eye. She sat down on the grassy bank near the clothesline and began to cry. Several of the younger hedgehogs began to sniff too.

Poor Mrs Hedgehog bent over to pick up her hat that she had left there since the morning and what do you think she saw?

Baby Hedgehog fast asleep! He must have crawled under his mother's hat and fallen asleep in the sun.

How the young hedgehogs cheered, they were so happy to find Baby Hedgehog. They made such a noise that their woodland friends nearby came out to join in the celebrations.

The Pink Elephant's Party

When Pink Elephant moved to Toy Town she was rather worried. "I hope I shall make new friends quickly," she said, as she unlocked the door to her new home.

At first Pink Elephant was busy settling in. She moved the furniture around until everything was exactly in the right place. Then, she put up brand new curtains, hung her favourite paintings on the walls, and filled all her vases with bunches of summer flowers.

"How lovely everything looks!" sighed Pink Elephant happily, and she sat down to admire her new home.

"It's very quiet in Toy Town," thought Pink Elephant, as she gazed out of the window into the empty street.

"I have an idea," she cried jumping up. "I'll give a party and invite everybody in the street. That way I will soon make friends."

So, there and then, Pink Elephant wrote out a huge pile of party invitations for the next afternoon. Then she ran up and down the street popping an envelope through every letter box.

The rest of the day Pink Elephant tidied her front garden. She mowed the lawn and swept the path. She polished the knocker on the front door and put the numbers back on the gate because they had fallen off.

Next morning, Pink Elephant got up very early and baked all kinds of lovely things to eat. After lunch, she decorated the house with balloons and coloured streamers. Last of all, she put on her party dress and then waited for her guests to arrive.

Pink Elephant waited and waited, but no-one came. She waited until it was past tea-time, but not one single guest arrived.

At last she opened her front door and walked down the garden path to the gate. What a surprise the Pink Elephant got! There were crowds of toys walking past with armfuls of presents and cards.

"Where are you all going?" shouted Pink Elephant, as they walked by.

"To Pink Elephant's party!" cried a furry rabbit as he waved the invitation in the air.

"But the party is here, at my house!" said Pink Elephant. "Why are you all walking past?"

"You live at Number 31," the rabbit answered, "and the invitation says Number 13."

"Oh dear!" gasped Pink Elephant. "I must have put the numbers back on my gate the wrong way round!"

How the toys laughed. They all crowded into Number 13. Pink Elephant gave a wonderful party and made lots of new friends.

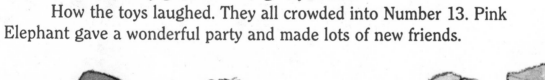

Ben's New Seat

Once upon a time, a grizzly bear called Ben made himself a seat.

"I'm rather lonely by myself in the forest," said Ben. "I shall sit here on my seat and see who passes by."

Very soon, along came a grey rabbit who hopped up onto Ben's knee. Then a squirrel jumped down from a branch overhead.

Two racoons who were scampering by, stopped when they saw Ben's seat, then jumped up on either side of him.

"Is there room for us?" asked a red fox and a stoat.

"And us?" squeaked a family of mice.

"It's a bit of a squeeze," shouted Ben. So everyone moved in tight and chattered together all afternoon.

They made such a noise that a tiny bluebird flew across to join in the fun. "Can I perch on your seat please?" the tiny bird asked Ben as he fluttered down.

Sadly, that was too much for Ben's new seat. It creaked and groaned and cracked. One by one the wooden legs snapped and everyone fell onto the ground laughing and giggling.

"Tomorrow I shall make a brand new seat, big enough for all my new friends," chuckled grizzly bear Ben, happily.

Three Jolly Fishermen

Once upon a time three jolly fishermen went to sea in a boat with a bright green sail.

The three jolly fishermen loved music and as they fished they sang. When the sea was calm and still, they sang quiet lullabies. When the boat bobbed up and down on the waves they sang jolly songs together. But when stormy winds blew and great waves crashed over their tiny boat, they sang opera as loud as they could.

Everyday the three jolly fisherman went out in their boat with the bright green sail, but they never ever caught a fish.

And this is the reason why!

The three jolly fisherman made such a noise that all the fish could hear them. As soon as they began to sing, every fish in the bay would gather under the boat with the bright green sail and sing along. The lobsters and crabs, all the fish and huge whales, joined a choir under the sea.

They were so busy singing together and learning new songs, they never ever got caught. And so none of them ended up on a plate for tea!

The Little Green Tractor

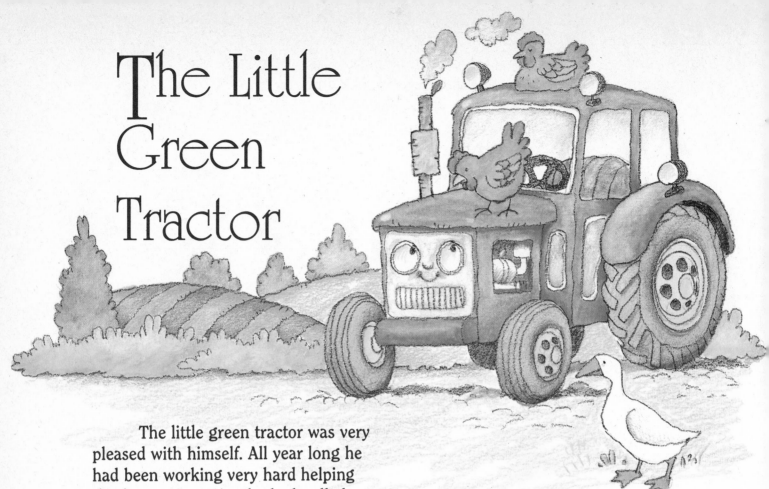

The little green tractor was very pleased with himself. All year long he had been working very hard helping the farmer. In spring he had pulled the plough and in summer he had taken all the hay back to the farm in his trailer. At harvest time he had carried so many loads of corn that all the farmer's barns were full for the winter.

"I think I shall go on holiday now!" said the little green tractor to the farmer. "I've worked very hard all year and I need a change!"

The farmer looked very puzzled. He had never heard of a tractor going on holiday before.

So early the next morning the little green tractor drove out of the farmyard, down the lane then turned left on to the main highway.

At first the road was quiet and the little green tractor chugged along happily. A few cars and vans drove past him and one or two lorry drivers waved as they went by.

On and on went the little green tractor until he came to a busy town. Here the road was filled with traffic and everyone was travelling very fast.

All of a sudden the cars, buses and trucks screeched to a halt at the traffic lights. But the little green tractor just carried on. (He had never seen a red light before, and didn't know he must stop!)

What a noise the other traffic made. They blew their horns so loudly at the little green tractor that he almost crashed.

As soon as he could, the frightened little green tractor turned off the main road into a garage and came to a stop.

"How I wish I was back home on the farm," said the little green tractor. "Now I shall never get home!"

As soon as the garage owner saw the little green tractor he was puzzled. "What on earth are you doing here?" he asked. "Have you lost your way?"

The little green tractor didn't know what to say.

"Our driver is taking a tanker full of fuel to your farm in five minutes. He'll give you a tow."

So that is how the little green tractor got safely back to the farm.

That night the farmer filled the little green tractor up with fuel and checked his engine. Then he gave the paintwork a polish until it shone.

Nothing was said about tractors going on holiday ever again!

The Bucket With A Hole

A small girl called Jane spent a week by the sea. She had a wonderful time. The weather was fine and the sea was warm and clear. Jane loved to carry water from the sea in her bright red bucket and then pour it into a deep hole she made with her spade. It was great fun!

On the very last day of her holiday, Jane found a hole in her bucket, then she noticed that the handle was loose.

"My bucket's no good any more!" said Jane sadly as she left it on the beach and went home.

"That's the end of me," said the bright red bucket as he lay forgotten on the sand.

A crab came over to try and cheer him up. "Something is bound to turn up," said the crab kindly, but still the bucket felt very miserable.

After a few days, a little boy came running across the beach. He saw the bright red bucket, but didn't mind that it had a hole and a broken handle. He shouted, "You're just what I need!" and picked up the bucket straight away.

The bucket and the little boy stayed together all summer long and when the little boy went home he took the bucket with him!

Archie Goes Visiting

Archie, the polar bear, lived in the Arctic, quite close to the North Pole. He didn't mind the freezing cold or the bitter winds at all because he had a coat of thick white fur to keep him warm. Archie could go for a swim in the ice-cold sea, then sit down on the ice and he didn't even shiver.

"I love living in the Arctic," said Archie, "except for one thing!"

"What's that then?" asked a Walrus, who had just scrambled up onto the ice.

"I have such a long way to walk to visit my polar bear friends!" said Archie with a sigh.

"How about going by air?" asked the Walrus, as he pointed to an aircraft that had just landed on the ice.

"I'm far too big to fit into one of those!" the polar bear laughed. "It would never take off!"

Just then, a team of huskies sped past pulling a sled. "Stop a minute!" yelled Archie, as he ran after them. "Can you give me a lift?" but the dogs just stuck out their tongues and ran even faster.

"I suppose I shall have to walk all the way as usual," sighed Archie, as he set off across the ice to visit his friends.

All of a sudden, something whizzed past him and pulled up at the explorers' camp over the hill.

"A snow mobile!" yelled Archie. "That's just what I need!"

The explorers were quite surprised when a polar bear knocked at their door. Archie asked in such a polite voice to borrow their snow mobile, they just couldn't refuse.

So if you ever visit the frozen lands quite close to the North Pole, and if you should happen to spot a polar bear whizzing across the ice on a snow mobile, it's likely to be Archie visiting his friends!

The Flying Mail

Everyone loves to hear the postman knocking at the door, especially when he has a letter for you.

Bertie Badger was the woodland postman. He had to walk a very long way to deliver his letters to houses all over the wood.

One day as he was sitting on a log having a rest and a cup of tea, a pigeon flew down to join him.

"Would you like some help?" he cooed.

Postman Badger laughed and gave the pigeon some of his sandwich. "You're a bit too small to be a postman."

Off flew the pigeon and very soon came back with some of his friends. When they saw Bertie Badger's sack they set to work straight away.

The smaller birds sorted the mail while the bigger birds carried the parcels between them.

Postman Badger watched in amazement. The birds came everyday to help deliver the mail on time and Postman Badger made extra sandwiches for them all - just to say thank you.

Texas Grandpa's Jeep

One day Texas Grandpa noticed that his Jeep had a flat front tyre. His grandson Pete went to the garage and pumped it up with the air hose.

Texas Grandpa talked so much that Pete forgot to switch off the hose. Now look at the tyre!

"Grandson Pete," shouted Texas Grandpa. "Pump up the other three!"

Now look at the jeep!

"That's just dandy!" yelled Texas Grandpa as he threw his hat high in the air.

"I've always wanted big wheels!"

Ordinary Street

Down Ordinary Street lived Mr Black. Mrs Grey lived just next door. Mr Brown lived on the other side, but the house next door to him was empty. No-one had lived there for a long time and the house had nothing inside.

One day Mrs White came to buy the house. "Oh dear! I couldn't live here!" she cried. "It's dusty and full of cobwebs." So she went away.

Next Mr Green came to look at the house. "The garden is far too small. There is no room for all my plants!" And he marched off down the street.

The following day Mrs Yellow arrived to look inside. "My goodness," she gasped, "it's far too dark. I need sunshine in every room!" And she drove off in her open car.

Now one dark day, when Ordinary Street was wet with rain, a truck full of noisy children came screeching round the corner.

Suddenly the rain clouds blew away, a patch of blue appeared in the sky and the sun shone brightly.

"We are the Rainbows," called the family to Mr Black, Mrs Grey and Mr Brown who were watching from their front doors.

"What a wonderful house!" gasped Mr and Mrs Rainbow and all the Rainbow children. I think we shall stay here for ever." And they did!

They painted the house in bright colours and filled the garden with beautiful flowers.

"I think," said Mr Black to Mr Grey. "we ought to do the same."

"I agree," nodded Mr Brown. So they started at once.

Soon the street looked so different that it didn't seem ordinary any more.

"Let's call it Bright Street." So they changed the name right away!

Mr Maggs And Monty

Little Mr Maggs had a big dog named Monty who loved to go for very long walks. Monty's legs were so long that little Mr Maggs had to run to keep up with him.

Every morning after breakfast, Monty would wait by the front door for little Mr Maggs to put on his hat and coat and take him out again.

They would walk all afternoon and come back home just in time for tea. Then after a quick snooze in front of the fire, Monty was ready to go out again.

Sometimes it was almost dark when they returned. Then little Mr Maggs would hang up Monty's lead and go straight to bed, quite tired out.

One morning after breakfast Monty went to the back door as usual, waiting to go for a walk. But little Mr Maggs put on his hat and coat and went out leaving Monty at home.

Little Mr Maggs hurried to the shops and came back with a mysterious parcel.

After lunch as usual, little Mr Maggs put on his hat and coat and put Monty's lead on him.

Soon they were both whizzing along. Monty ran faster and faster, but still Mr Maggs kept up. Monty couldn't understand why!

At last poor Monty had to stop for a rest and when he looked round, he saw that little Mr Maggs was wearing ROLLER SKATES!

That is what was in the mysterious parcel.

Tom and Peter bought two big balloons. Tom's balloon was red and Peter's balloon was blue.

The next day as Tom was looking out of his bedroom window, he saw a big blue balloon.

The Big Blue Balloon

"That must be Peter!" laughed naughty Tom. "I'll burst his big blue balloon!" So, very quietly, Tom opened the window, and using a sharp pin he burst the big blue balloon. It went off with a very loud bang.

That made Tom laugh even more. Straight away there was a loud knocking on Tom's door. He ran downstairs at once, and from behind the front door a very big voice boomed, "Who burst my big blue balloon?"

Now Tom had some quick thinking to do!

29

What A Strange House!

"What a lovely morning," said Lottie, as she opened the front door. "I think I shall go for a ride on my bike." So she ran upstairs to find her shorts.

When she opened the shed door, Lottie got quite a surprise. "Someone has been very busy in here!" she cried, then ran outside to find her grandad.

Two blackbirds had built a nest in the basket on the front of her bike. "No more bike rides for you for a while!" chuckled Grandad.

"What a strange house for blackbirds," giggled Lottie. "I'll go for a walk and see what else I can find."

When Lottie called at the cottage down the lane, she found that two swallows had built a nest in the front porch. Everyone would have to use the back door for a few weeks.

Later she called at the farm on the hill and she saw a duck sitting on six eggs. Lottie could hardly believe her eyes, the nest was on the farmer's old tractor seat!

Next she met her friend from school who had just found a robin's nest in a plant pot.

Then a lady called her over to see some mice nesting in a garden chair.

"What strange houses I've seen today!" said Lottie as she ran past the mill.

"Come in and see our new kittens, they've made their home in a barrel," shouted the miller's wife.

Lottie rushed inside and bent down to find six tiny kittens fast asleep in an old flour barrel.

"I have a surprise for you Lottie," whispered the miller's wife in her ear. "Your grandad has asked you to choose two kittens for your very own, and take them back home today!"

How carefully Lottie walked back home, with her two kittens tucked up in a shopping basket.

Her grandad was smiling as he opened the back door. "Now where are you going to keep those Lottie?"

As soon as she put the basket on the floor, both kittens jumped out and ran straight into Lottie's dolls' house.

"What a strange house for two kittens," laughed Lottie. "Welcome to your new home!"

As for the kittens, they were already fast asleep.

The Lonely Monkey

Far away across a bright blue ocean was a tiny desert island. Everyday the sun shone down on the sandy beach and warmed the clear waters around the shore.

In the middle of this island grew tall palm trees full of coconuts and banana plants loaded with bunches of ripe bananas.

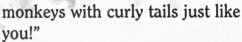

And who do you think lived in this wonderful place? Just one little brown monkey with a curly tail.

"I'm so lonely, I wish I had a friend!" said the monkey out loud as he sat on the beach. But he knew there was no-one to hear him.

A brilliant coloured fish swimming by, stuck his head out of the water. "Follow me and swim to the next island. It's full of little brown monkeys with curly tails just like you!"

"But I can't swim," cried the monkey. "Please fish, will you teach me how?"

"Certainly!" replied the fish. "Just walk into the water and do as I say."

So the little brown monkey walked slowly into the sea.

"Now take your feet off the bottom and move your arms," cried the fish.

"Oh dear!" shrieked the monkey. "I don't like this one bit! Swimming is far too wet."

The brightly coloured fish just laughed and swam away, while the monkey dried on the sand.

Now standing on the beach was a great white pelican. "Come with me and fly to the island. I'm taking off right now!"

"But I can't fly," cried the monkey. "Please pelican, will you teach me how?"

"Certainly!" replied the pelican. "Climb on top of the tallest palm tree, flap your arms and fly away!"

The monkey did as the pelican had said, but he fell with a thud onto the sand, and some of the coconuts fell on top of him. When he looked up the pelican had flown away.

All of a sudden the little monkey leapt to his feet. "I know!" he shouted out loud. "I'll chop down the coconut trees and the huge banana plants and make a raft." He jumped up and down with glee. "I shall sail across to the other island and make friends with the other monkeys."

"What a very silly idea," said a voice from the sea. The little brown monkey looked up to see a small turtle walking slowly up the beach. "Chop down all the trees and you'll have nothing to eat and neither will anyone else."

The monkey hung his head. "I don't have an axe!" he muttered.

"Just as well!" the turtle said, shaking his head. "I could take you across to the island on my back, but you're far too big." And with that the

small green turtle walked slowly back into the sea.

This made the little brown monkey feel so sad and lonely, that he sat on the sand and cried.

Then all of a sudden, out of the sea, rose the biggest turtle you have ever seen. Very slowly he plodded towards the sad little brown monkey.

"Dry those tears, climb onto my back and don't forget to hold on tight," said the big turtle with a smile. "You'll never be lonely again when we reach the other island."

The turtle's shell looked so

large, the little monkey knew he would be quite safe.

When the little brown monkey looked down into the clear blue sea, what do you think he saw? Bobbing up and down in the water next to them was the little green turtle.

"I knew I was far too small to carry you to the island, so I asked my great great grandfather to help you. He's very kind and very wise."

"So are you," said the monkey with a smile. "Thank you for everything, little green turtle. I shall never be lonely again."

A Shelf Full Of Dolls

Sarah's daddy had a job at the airport. Most of the time he went to work in the morning and came home every night. But sometimes he flew away to different countries and stayed there for a few days.

Every time he came back from a trip abroad, Sarah's daddy brought her a doll. She had a different doll from every country he visited!

Sarah's daddy had put up some shelves on Sarah's bedroom wall so that she could look at her collection of dolls all the time. One day he added a new shelf next to the others.

"All ready for the new doll I'll be bringing back from my next trip!" he said.

"It's a very long shelf for one doll!" said Sarah, looking puzzled as she waved her daddy goodbye.

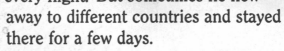

After a week, Daddy returned and brought Sarah the new doll he had promised. And what a strange doll it was. It had no arms or legs, it was made of painted wood and rattled!

"This is a Russian doll," Daddy smiled, as he unscrewed its body and found another doll inside.

Then Sarah unscrewed the second doll and found another. On and on she went until there were nine beautiful Russian dolls, each one a little bit smaller than the other.

"Now I know why you put up such a long shelf!" laughed Sarah, as she placed the dolls in a row.

The Professor's Pencil

Jack lived next door to Professor Smart, who spent all day and most of the night inventing things!

"I wish you could invent something to help me," said Jack with a grin, as he sat outside on the step practising his handwriting in an exercise book.

"I most certainly can!" replied the Professor, and he rushed off to start work straight away.

All that day and most of the next, Jack could hear rattling and banging coming from next door.

"Finished at last!" cried the Professor from over the fence. Jack jumped up at once and ran round to his house to take a look. There in the garden was the strangest machine Jack had ever seen.

"What is that?" asked Jack in amazement.

"A machine for making full stops!" said the Professor with pride.

Jack laughed until he cried. "But I can do that easily with one small pencil."

"Oh dear!" sighed the Professor. "Of course you can, what a silly man I am!"

"Never mind," said Jack smiling, "your machine will be perfect for planting Dad's seeds!"

36

Ossie's Umbrella

Every morning Ossie the ostrich went for a run across the plain. Now, as you know, ostriches can run very fast indeed, but they cannot fly.

Ossie really wanted to fly. "If I run fast enough, one day I may take off and fly up into the air," he thought. Sad to say, he never did!

One fine morning, after a long hard run, Ossie the ostrich stopped for a rest. As he looked down on the ground he spotted a brightly coloured snake.

"Lovely morning for a run!" giggled Ossie, because he knew that snakes never ran anywhere.

When the snake didn't reply, Ossie felt a bit ashamed. "I was only teasing," he said as he bent down to the snake. "Sorry."

Suddenly Ossie heard loud laughter, it was a little rhino who had stopped to see what was happening. "It's not a snake, you silly ostrich, it's an umbrella!"

As Ossie opened the umbrella and held it high above his head, a strong breeze blew over the plain and gently lifted the startled ostrich into the air.

"I'm flying," gasped Ossie. "I'm really flying!"

37

The animals below got such a shock as they looked up and saw an ostrich gliding above the tree tops.

A startled crane flew beside Ossie for a while. "Never thought I'd see an ostrich fly," he called. "I'm off to tell my friends about this."

Ossie the ostrich flew around happily all day and when the wind dropped, he floated gently to the ground.

"That was really exciting!" gasped Ossie as he carefully folded up the umbrella. "I shall carry this wherever I go, and when the wind blows I shall be off on another flying adventure!"

39

The Big Wooden Toy Box

Tom and Rosie-Anne had a great big toy box. It was made of wood, with a lid that made a very loud bang when you closed it!

The toy box was so large that every single one of Tom and Rosie-Anne's toys fitted inside. This is why the children's room was always so tidy and neat.

Their mother loved the wooden toy box, but the toys did not!

"I don't like being in here one little bit!" said the rag doll to one of the soft toys. "The skipping rope gets tangled round my legs, and I have bricks and jigsaw pieces sticking into my back."

"That sounds very painful," whispered one of the teddies, "but what I hate most of all is the dark, when the lid is closed it's very spooky in here!"

"Perhaps if we all pushed hard we could manage to open the lid," suggested the clown. But the lid was far too heavy, so the toys had to stay in the dark.

One Saturday Tom and Rosie-Anne asked their mother if she had a job for them to do.

"Not at the moment," she said, "but Dad may find you one in the garage."

Dad was delighted and found them a job straight away. "Can you tidy up my tools and put them away in those boxes?"

"What a mess!" cried the children as they looked around the garage. Tools were scattered all over the floor and piled up under benches.

"I wish I had your big wooden toy box!" said their dad with a sigh. "All my tools would fit inside, and when I closed the lid, everything would look tidy."

This gave Tom and Rosie-Anne an idea. "Will you swap all your small tool boxes for our big wooden one?" the children asked.

"I certainly will!" he agreed at once. "We'll do it straight away."

When the job was finished, everyone was happy. Dad had the big wooden toy box with the lid and his garage was never untidy again.

Tom and Rosie-Anne could still keep their room as tidy as ever, and they could see their toys all the time.

As for the toys, they had much more room, they could look around and they were never shut in the dark again.

Fluffy The Tortoise

Grandad had always told Lottie that when the top of her fluffy hat reached the top of the gate she could have a pet!

"Whoopie!" cried Lottie, "I know exactly what I want."

"Come with me to my hen house," said Grandad. "I have a hen with six fluffy chicks. Would you like one of those?"

"They're lovely!" said Lottie, "but I know exactly what I want."

"At the bottom of the garden is a duck with five yellow ducklings. How about one of those?"

"They're great!" said Lottie, "but I know exactly what I want!"

Along came the postwoman with the letters. "I have a cat with three soft kittens. You can choose one of those."

"That's terrific!" said Lottie, "but I know exactly what I want."

Next came the baker bringing the bread. "My dog has four little puppies at home. You can pick one of those if you like."

"How marvellous!" said Lottie, "but I know exactly what I want."

The farmer across the field owned a pony with foals. "Come and take a look, you might like one of those."

"They are beautiful!" said Lottie, "but I know exactly what I want."

In a sty on the farm was a pig with ten little piglets.
"Goodness!" said Lottie. "I couldn't manage even one of those, I know exactly what I want."

Then she went to the pet shop. The man inside said, "Have a good look round before you choose."

"Wonderful!" cried Lottie, "I have found exactly what I want. I want a tortoise!"

Just then a parrot pulled off Lottie's fluffy hat. It dropped right on top of the tortoise.

"Perfect!" cried Lottie, "I shall call you Fluffy the Tortoise. And you are exactly what I want."

43

Hilda The Hippo

Hilda the hippo lived on the bank of a wide muddy river. All the other hippos liked the edge of the river best, where the mud was thick and sticky like warm melted chocolate. They even dozed off to sleep in it on hot afternoons, with the top of their heads just showing above the mud.

"Come on in!" cried the rest of Hilda's family. "The mud is lovely!" But Hilda was not keen on the idea at all, she liked standing in the clean, refreshing rain, especially during a thunderstorm. Best of all she loved to watch the frogs leaping onto the lily-pads and floating on top of the water.

"I wish I could do that," Hilda sighed. "Then I would never get muddy!" But each time Hilda tried to fit all four feet onto a lily-pad, she sank like a stone!

Now frogs can be very helpful creatures and full of good ideas. So one day, they pushed a lily-pad under each one of Hilda's back feet and gave her two long poles to help her along. With a bit of practise, Hilda was soon skiing across the water on her lily-pad skis.

It so happened that one day a photographer took Hilda's picture and sent it to a wildlife magazine. Very soon, everyone wanted to see Hilda, the skiing hippo.

"In my country," the photographer told Hilda, "everyone skis all the time! Why don't you come and see for yourself?"

So Hilda left her muddy river and flew far away on an aeroplane. It was very exciting!

When she landed, the little hippo couldn't believe her eyes. Everywhere was white! Mountains, hills, even streets were covered in thick, fluffy, white snow.

In no time at all, Hilda jumped on a pair of skis and whizzed off down the mountain side. In and out of the trees she sped until she came to an enormous ski jump. Hilda took off, flew through the air, then made a perfect landing at the bottom.

"What a winner!" yelled the crowd. "It's the longest jump ever made!" They gave Hilda a shiny, gold medal.

Hilda stayed a while to ski in the snowy land, and when she returned on the aeroplane, she wore her gold medal around her neck - just to show the frogs on the muddy river back home!

45

The Mole's Adventure

"What a lovely morning," purred Ginger the cat as he stepped outside the front door. "I think I shall take a stroll round the garden."

So Ginger walked down the path, past the flower bed, then walked back again along the top of the fence.

"That's enough exercise for one morning," said Ginger out loud, and jumped down onto the grass.

All of a sudden, a small mound of earth appeared right next to him. "Goodness me," gasped Ginger, "where did that come from?" From the middle of the earth popped a velvety brown mole.

"Good morning to you!" the Mole said with a grin. "I've just come up from my underground burrow in search of an adventure!"

Ginger jumped back up onto the fence in surprise. "What sort of adventure would you like?" he asked the Mole.

"I want to climb up on the fence just like you," laughed the Mole. "Better still, I would like to climb a tree!"

"Moles can't climb trees," said Ginger with a shake of his head, "but that would be an adventure for you. Just let me think for a minute!"

So Ginger sat on the fence, closed his eyes and thought and thought.

At last he came up with a wonderful idea which he whispered to the Mole.

Behind the fence were two apple trees and on the lowest branch of one was a swing. Ginger helped the Mole up onto the seat and pushed it until he was swinging higher and higher. Then, quick as a wink, Ginger ran up the other tree and grabbed the Mole as he swung near to him.

The two then sat side by side on one of the branches. "Now you have climbed a tree!" laughed Ginger.

"What a great adventure!" gasped the Mole, quite out of breath.

Soon a small crowd gathered under the apple tree. "Look!" they shouted pointing up at the branch, "a Mole that can climb trees!"

How the two new friends laughed. "Perhaps someone will take our picture," said Ginger, "then you will be able to show everyone how you once really did climb a tree!"

Let's Go On A Picnic

One fine, warm summer's day a few of the woodland folk discussed going on a day out.

"It's a perfect day for a picnic," said the fox, as he gazed up at the clear blue sky.

"Why don't we pack a picnic basket and go on a hike?" suggested two chipmunks, who were always very helpful.

Everyone agreed it was a splendid idea, and ran back home to fetch some food.

In next to no time, the animals were back and the picnic basket full to the brim.

"This basket is rather heavy," said a rabbit, as he tried to lift one corner.

"We can take turns carrying it," suggested one of the helpful chipmunks, "we'll take the first turn!"

So the friends set off. They walked through the wood, down a lane, then across a meadow until they came to a stream.

"Look at that lovely place over there, it's just perfect for a picnic," called the porcupine, as he pointed to a field across the water.

"But how are we going to get across?" cried the animals all together.

"Look, a log has fallen across the stream!" cried the two chipmunks, helpful as ever.

"I'll go first," said the fox. "I have a perfect sense of balance."

"Me next," said the porcupine, who couldn't keep his balance at all. "If I slip, I shall fall onto the rabbits!"

"Oh no you won't!" cried the rabbits hopping in front. One by one they crossed the log with great care. How funny the five looked as they wobbled their way along the log trying to keep balance.

Now while all this was going on, the two helpful little chipmunks had been very busy. Believe it or not, the animals' picnic was already set out in the opposite field.

The chipmunks had noticed that the fallen log was hollow. It was quite big enough for them to scamper through and carry all the picnic food to the other side. The rabbits, the porcupine and the fox could have gone through the log quite easily, instead of wobbling their way across!

At last the five friends reached the other side of the stream and flopped down on the grass with relief. And what do you think they found? The two chipmunks sitting by the side of the picnic, helpless with laughter!

Later on when the picnic was over, everybody went back through the hollow log with no trouble at all!

The two little chipmunks led the way, and helpful as ever, carried the empty picnic basket back home.

Matilda Is Missing

Matilda went everywhere with Maggie. Matilda was Maggie's favourite doll and when Maggie went out, she took Matilda with her zipped up safely in her own special bag.

One day Maggie went for a walk across the park with Matilda's zip-bag slung over her shoulder.

"How about a swing?" Maggie asked as she unzipped Matilda's special bag.

Poor Maggie gasped! The bag was empty! She yelled at the top of her voice. "Matilda is missing!"

She shouted so loudly that everyone in the park could hear. In fact, Maggie's voice was so noisy, that everyone in the town could hear her too.

Even Maggie's mother could hear her cry, "Matilda is missing!" although she was inside the house.

As fast as possible, Maggie's mother ran upstairs and saw there Matilda the doll sitting on Maggie's bed. She had slipped from the bag and was safe at home all the time.

"What a silly girl I am!" said Maggie when she found out, and her face went very red indeed!

The Lonely Little Lighthouse

In the middle of the sea, perched safely on top of the rocks, stood a little lighthouse. His light shone far out to sea, but no ship had passed by for years. So one day, the lighthouse keeper said goodbye and left him all alone.

This made the little lighthouse feel very sad. "I'm no use to anyone anymore," he sobbed. "My light will soon go out and I'll be forgotten!"

Now some of the seals and walruses who visited the rocks heard the lonely lighthouse. So they put their heads together, and very soon thought of a way to cheer him up.

"We can take it in turns to be the lighthouse keeper and work the light!" suggested the biggest walrus.

The little lighthouse liked the sound of this and began to brighten up right away.

So every night, when darkness falls over the sea, the little lighthouse shines his light. Then the dolphins, the seals and the walruses, sometimes even a couple of whales, come out to play.

Everyone has a wonderful time, especially the little lighthouse. His light shines in the dark like a star and he is never ever lonely.

Jolly Monster's Birthday

It was Jolly Monster's birthday and he was giving a great big birthday party. All his monster friends had been invited and Jolly Monster was hoping for some very large presents, but what he wanted most of all was a big surprise.

That afternoon when the Jolly Monster's friends arrived for tea, each one was carrying a great big box. Jolly Monster could hardly wait to open them.

In the first box was an enormous pair of trainers with red laces.

"I could run a marathon in these!" chuckled Jolly Monster.

When he opened the next box, he found a tee-shirt, not quite the right size!

Most of his friends had brought useful things, like a huge pairs of socks, gigantic gloves, but he received a hat that was far too small!

Some brought games and large balloons that could be seen from far away.

There were sacks full of sweets and lollipops as tall as trees.

All of a sudden someone yelled, "Hide your eyes Jolly Monster, here comes the big surprise!"

Speeding across the lawn came a lorry loaded down with....what do you think?

The biggest blow up castle you have ever seen. Just perfect for Jolly Monster and his friends to bounce up and down on all day!

"I wished for a big surprise, and this is just perfect!" laughed Jolly Monster, as he jumped up into the air.

53

Bobby Gets Dressed

Little Bobby Briggs was a very good boy, except for one thing. He would not get dressed in the morning!

When the alarm clock rang at eight o'clock, Bobby would jump out of bed straight away, run to the bathroom, wash, clean his teeth and comb his hair but - he would not get dressed in the morning!

This made everyone very cross as well as very late.

One day his sister Susie thought of a good idea. She put all Bobby's clothes for that day into a pillow case and then played his favourite tune on his toy xylophone.

"When the music stops," Susie told her little brother, "take something out of the pillow case and put it on!"

Bobby thought this was a great game and couldn't wait to join in.

First he took out his hat, and when the music stopped again he put on a sock. Next came his sweater, then another sock, then pants and a shirt and very soon he was dressed to go out.

What a good idea sister Susie! Are you going to play this game with Bobby every time he goes out?

Racing Rabbit

A postcard came one day for Wise Rabbit. It was from his long lost cousins who lived half way across the world.

'Do come and visit us as soon as you can,' the message read. Wise Rabbit thought this a good idea.

"It's rather a long way," Wise Rabbit said, "but if I can find someone to mow my lawn and look after my garden shed, I shall go at once!"

The neighbours said, "Ask any one of us to mow your lawn and look after your garden shed, but whatever you do, don't ask Bunny Hopkins!"

This made Wise Rabbit think long and hard.

The very next day when Bunny Hopkins passed by, Wise Rabbit gave him the key to the garden shed.

"Leave everything to me!" said Bunny Hopkins eagerly. "I will mow your lawn every week and guard your garden shed with my life."

Off went Wise Rabbit to visit his cousins, but sadly, Bunny Hopkins did not keep his promise.

All summer long he sat in the garden sunbathing. The grass on the lawn grew tall and the weeds almost covered the garden shed.

"I think it's about time I mowed the lawn!" said Bunny Hopkins with a yawn.

When at last the young rabbit unlocked the garden shed, he was in for a big surprise! For standing next to the mower was the biggest motorbike he had ever seen.

On top of the seat was a note which read, 'When you have finished mowing the lawn, use my bike as often as you like.'

Poor Bunny Hopkins just stood and stared. "If I'd mowed the lawn each week as I'd promised, I could have ridden the bike all summer!" he cried.

How quickly Bunny Hopkins got to work, and at last when all the jobs were finished, he raced off on Wise Rabbit's magnificent motorbike.

"Soon Wise Rabbit will be back," sighed Bunny Hopkins, "and I won't be able to ride the motorbike ever again!"

But on the very day he was due to return, Bunny Hopkins received a postcard. It was from Wise Rabbit!

The card was addressed to 'Bunny Hopkins, The Racing Rabbit', and this is what it said: 'I am going to stay here until next year. Please mow my lawn, look after my garden shed and don't forget to ride my motorbike!' Bunny Hopkins was delighted.

Terry's First Prize

Terry drove a yellow taxi all day long. The city streets were very busy with lots of noisy traffic, which often gave Terry a headache. "Sometimes I wish I lived in a place with no cars at all," he sighed.

One day a man knocked on Terry's door. "You have won first prize in our great competition!"

Terry looked pleased. "Is it a desert island?" he asked the man.

"I'll give you a clue!" the man smiled. "It has four wheels and travels on the road."

Terry's face fell. "I hope it's not a car!" he cried. He soon cheered up when he saw his very own gipsy caravan!

Mrs Bruno's Pies

Mrs Bruno baked marvellous hot cherry pies. They tasted so good that everyone wanted to buy them. Before long Mrs Bruno's hot cherry pies became famous.

"What am I going to do?" asked Mrs Bruno, looking worried. "I love to bake cherry pies, but when I stop to answer the door, the pies in the oven get burnt, and I have so far to walk to my customers, that my pies are cold by the time they are delivered."

What a problem!

"I think I shall have to stop baking my hot cherry pies!"

"What! No more pies?" cried the customers. So they got together and came up with a splendid idea. They would come and collect the pies from Mrs Bruno's house.

Now Mrs Bruno can bake her famous hot cherry pies, and everyone is happy!

The Musical Mouse

Morgan the mouse made no noise at all. "You really are as quiet as a mouse Morgan!" everyone said with a smile.

"Mice are naturally quiet creatures," nodded Morgan wisely. Then he scampered off without so much as a rustle or a squeak.

Now one day, as Morgan was sitting perfectly still by the side of the road, he heard a wonderful sound. As he listened the sound grew louder and louder.

"It's coming nearer!" shouted Morgan at the top of his voice, which was very unlike him.

Just then the town band came round the corner playing catchy tunes on their instruments.

Morgan had never heard music before and knew he had to join in.

"I've been so quiet all my life," yelled Morgan as he ran alongside the players, "I want to make a great big noise!"

"Try these cymbals," said the cat. Morgan crashed them together so hard that the band almost fell over one another.

"Try this trombone," suggested the dog. Morgan played so hard he almost blew the band away.

Next he tried the drums and made such a noise that the elephants ran behind a wall in fright.

"I thought mice were supposed to be quiet creatures!" whispered one of the band.

"We are!" Morgan agreed as he banged hard on a tambourine, "but making a noise is such wonderful fun!"

By now the band was in a muddle. They were playing different tunes and everyone was bumping into each other.

Suddenly the band leader shouted above the din. "You can be leader of the band Morgan, then everybody can get back to making music instead of a noise!"

Honey Bear's Promise

Honey Bear was very fond of sweet things to eat. He loved jam and candy bars, sticky gingerbread and sugary biscuits - but most of all he loved honey! Every morning, he spread it thickly on hot toast. At lunch time he let it trickle all over his pancakes, and at tea he gobbled up a huge plateful of tasty honey sandwiches.

Now Mother Bear kept the honey on the very top shelf of the kitchen cupboard. The shelf was far too high for Honey Bear to reach unless he climbed to the top of Father's wooden steps.

One day, when he thought no-one was looking, Honey Bear carried Father's wooden steps into the kitchen.

"If I'm very quiet and ever so careful, I can climb up and reach the honey jar from the top shelf," Honey Bear chuckled to himself. But when Honey Bear got almost to the top, the steps began to wobble and shake which gave the little bear quite a fright.

"Help! Help!" yelled Honey Bear as he clung onto the steps.

Luckily, Father Bear was behind the kitchen door and caught Honey Bear before he fell off and hurt himself.

Father Bear looked very cross."You must promise never to climb the steps," he said sternly, "it's far too dangerous!"

Honey Bear hung his head and promised.

The very next day when Honey Bear looked longingly at that big jar of honey, he remembered his promise. Then all of a sudden he had a wonderful idea. "I know how to reach the honey, without using Father's steps at all!"

So very carefully he opened the bottom drawer of the cupboard, then the next drawer, and the next, and so on, until he could reach that tempting jar of honey.

Honey Bear slowly climbed down with the precious jar tucked safely in his paw. He reached for a spoon from the top drawer of the cupboard, then settled down to enjoy the lovely honey!

The Runaround Clock

The alarm clock on the bedroom shelf opened his eyes and looked around. Dawn was breaking and the first rays of the sun were just peeping through the curtains.

"I'm bored!" the clock ticked. "Everyone is still fast asleep. I've been ticking away all through the night, and no-one has listened to a single tic-toc!"

"That's what clocks are supposed to do!" snapped a china dog on the shelf, "just tic-toc away all night and all day."

"Well, it's very boring!" replied the alarm clock crossly. "No-one listens to me until eight o'clock when my alarm bell rings!"

The alarm clock looked down at his hands. "It's only five o'clock. I think I shall go for a run." And with that he jumped off the shelf and ran downstairs.

Once outside, the alarm clock dashed off quickly down the street. He hadn't gone very far when a small dog, out for his early morning walk, barked and growled at the poor alarm clock. The dog chased him across the road, where a boy delivering newspapers almost ran over him with his bicycle wheel.

Then, without any warning, a machine that cleans the street, sprayed him with cold water and whisked him along the gutter with its whurring brushes.

"Oh dear me!" gasped the alarm clock, looking down at his hands. "It's six o'clock. I've only been outside an hour. How I wish I was back on the shelf at home."

But there was worse to come! The man who drove the dustcart saw the alarm clock upside down in the gutter. He thought it was a piece of junk and threw him onto his cart!

The dustcart travelled round the streets for ages collecting more and more rubbish. At last the alarm clock struggled to the top of the pile and peered out of the back of the cart.

To his great delight he was only two doors away from his own house, so he jumped down from the cart and rolled into his very own garden.

The cat, who had been out all night, sniffed at the alarm clock, then pushed him over with her paw.

"Look at the time!" gasped the alarm clock as he looked at his hands. "It's almost five minutes to eight!"

With one last effort he ran upstairs, jumped back on bedroom shelf and rang his bell as hard as he could.

"Time to get up!" cried one of the family. "It's exactly eight o'clock and our alarm clock is right on time as usual!"

Who Has Eaten The Garden?

In spring (when the weather begins to turn warm), Lottie and Grandma spent hours planting vegetable seeds in the garden.

Lottie thought they took ages to grow, but one morning in summer Grandma said that at last they were ready for picking.

"Let's have peas today!" said Lottie. "They're my favourite!"

So she took a bowl into the garden and filled it with fresh green pea-pods. Then she sat outside the kitchen door and shelled the peas for lunch - perhaps she ate one or two as well!

The next day Lottie chose carrots for lunch, but when she went out to pick them, she found that something had been nibbling the garden. Most of the vegetables had been eaten! Whatever could it be?

"It must be rabbits!" said the milkman. "They love carrots."

"It can't be," said Lottie. "I give them plenty of lettuce and cabbage leaves!"

"It must be pigeons!" said the postman. "They love peas."

"Never!" cried Lottie. "I give them corn and crumbs all the time."

"Then, it's slugs!" said the boy returning from school. "They'll eat anything."

"Oh dear!" sighed Lottie. "What shall we do?"

"Make a scarecrow," suggested Grandad. "We'll do it this afternoon."

Next morning, as soon as it was light, Lottie crept downstairs and tiptoed into the vegetable garden. What a surprise she got! Not rabbits, not pigeons or even slugs - but a baby deer nibbling beans and making friends with the scarecrow.

Very quietly, Lottie crept up to the deer and stroked his nose. "So it was you who ate the garden," she whispered. "I wish I could keep you as a pet."

Grandad shook his head. "I'm sure if you put out some food, the little deer will come out of the wood to see you sometimes," he said with a smile. "As long as he leaves our vegetables alone!"

The Animal Olympics

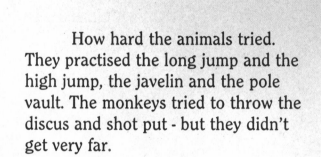

Once a year the animals held a meeting. They talked about this and that, told one another all their news, then everyone joined in a gigantic party.

Now this year they wanted to do something quite different, so they decided to hold the Animal Olympics!

"We'll all meet back here one week from now," suggested the elephant. "Then everyone can take part and try to win a gold medal."

"How exciting!" cried all the animals, and they ran off at once to practise.

How hard the animals tried. They practised the long jump and the high jump, the javelin and the pole vault. The monkeys tried to throw the discus and shot put - but they didn't get very far.

"I'm the fastest animal in the world," sobbed Cheetah. "If I take part I shall win all the races, and it will be no fun at all!"

"Cheer up!" said the Hippo. "I have the perfect job for a fast runner like you. Will you carry the Olympic torch and start the games?"

The cheetah was delighted and stopped crying at once.

The day of the Animal Olympic Games came at last. The animals arrived looking very smart in their sports clothes, all except one. Tommy Tortoise stood on his own looking very sad. "I've practised everyday, but I'm far too slow to take part in any event," he sobbed.

"Not to worry!" said the Hippo. "We need someone to fire the starting pistol and time the races."

Tommy Tortoise cheered up at once and plodded off to the starting point.

All of a sudden, one of the other animals began sniffing. It was the cheetah.

"Why are you crying too?" asked the Hippo rather surprised.

At last the Animal Olympics began. They lasted all day long, and each animal won a medal for one event or another.

Everyone went home late that evening feeling very happy and very tired - especially the tortoise and the cheetah!

The Rocky Mountain Train

Once upon a time there was a Red Train which carried people across the Rocky Mountains.

Everyday the Red Train had to pull lots of carriages, because so many people wanted to cross the mountains to the other side. Slowly, the Red Train huffed and puffed his way over the mountains with his load getting heavier and heavier everyday.

"My goodness!" said the engine driver, when he saw more and more

In the rain and frost and snow.
The bright Red Train will be our guide,
Until we reach the other side.
Merrily he'll puff along,
Until we end this happy song!"

One morning, there were even more people than usual waiting at the station. Very soon the Red Train's carriages were packed full of passengers.

The Red Train pulled very

people waiting at the station each morning. "If I add any more carriages, the Red Train will break down one day!"

Now the Red Train kept going because he liked to make the passengers happy, and he loved to listen to the song they sang on the journey across the Rocky Mountains.

"Through the mountain we will go,

slowly out of the station, but as soon as he started to cross the mountains, he huffed and puffed, blew his whistle and came to a stop.

"Poor Red Train," said his engine driver. "He's too tired to go any further!"

"Oh dear!" cried all the passengers. "This is our fault. What can we do?"

All of a sudden a little boy jumped down from the train and shouted to the passengers leaning out of the carriage windows.

"The song we always sing says '*through* the mountains we will go', perhaps the Red Train used to go through the mountains and there is a hidden tunnel somewhere - that would save going up and over them!"

The Red Train blew his whistle very hard, he could just remember going through the tunnel many years ago.

At once the passengers climbed out of the train, they searched round the mountain until at last they found the opening of the old tunnel.

Everyone worked very hard pulling away tangled undergrowth and clearing the track.

Very soon the Red Train was speeding happily through the tunnel, straight through the mountains in next to no time. The passengers sang the Red Train's very own song at the tops of their voices!

Jed's Special Sweater

One afternoon Jed's great aunt Jenny came to his house for tea. Jed liked his great aunt Jenny because she was kind and funny, and had a very special wrist watch that played 'Happy Birthday' even if it wasn't your birthday that day!

After tea, Great Aunt Jenny asked Jed if she could borrow a book about space travel. Jed had lots, so he gave her a book full of pictures of spacemen, rockets and the moon.

Next time Great Aunt Jenny came to tea she was carrying a brown paper parcel.

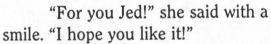

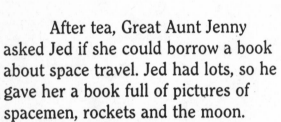

"For you Jed!" she said with a smile. "I hope you like it!"

Inside the parcel Jed found a lovely bright red sweater. On the front Great Aunt Jenny had carefully knitted a picture of a spaceman in his helmet, with a silver rocket in the background.

"Just like the picture in your book," laughed Great Aunt Jenny as Jed pulled on his wonderful sweater.

He was delighted with his present and wanted to wear it everyday. He tried very hard not to get it dirty, because he missed his sweater so much when it had to be washed.

Every Thursday Jed and his school friends went to the swimming pool with their teacher. After the swimming lesson, all the children rushed into the changing rooms to get dried and dressed.

"Quick as you can, children!" called their teacher. "The bus is waiting to take you back to school."

Quickly Jed pulled on his clothes, tied his shoes, then hunted round for his special sweater. At last he spotted it under a bench on the wet floor. Fast as he could, Jed tugged on his sweater, then hurried onto the bus with all the others.

Later that afternoon, as Jed was walking home, he looked down at his sweater and got quite a shock. The front was plain red and the spacemen with his rocket had vanished.

"Oh no!" gasped poor Jed, almost in tears. "I must have put on the wrong sweater!"

When he got home Great Aunt Jenny was there. "I've lost my spaceman sweater," sobbed Jed.

All of a sudden Great Aunt Jenny began to smile and Jed's mother laughed out loud.

"Your sweater's back to front," giggled Great Aunt Jenny. "Come here, you silly boy," and she turned Jed's sweater around, so the spaceman and the rocket were at the front for everyone to see!

Teddy's Soup

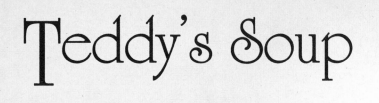

Teddy Bear had a problem, he was very bad at spelling.

"I do try really hard!" he told Mother Bear. "In fact, I am busy reading my book right now."

Mother Bear smiled to herself when she noticed that Teddy was holding his book upside down.

Then she thought of a bright idea. Mother Bear went into the kitchen straight away and made Teddy a large bowl of alphabet soup.

"Now you can learn your letters as you eat," she laughed.

The alphabet tasted so good, that Teddy emptied the bowl in one gulp.

"Perhaps that wasn't such a good idea after all," chuckled Mother Bear, as she filled Teddy's bowl up with soup once more!

Cathy's Tea Party

One afternoon, deep down at the bottom of the ocean, Cathy the crab was giving a tea party.

That morning she had made lots of iced buns, a very fancy cake and two huge plates of seaweed sandwiches.

In the afternoon when she laid the table, Cathy set out eight plates and eight cups and saucers.

"How many guests are coming to the tea party?" asked a cheeky little fish passing by.

"I've invited one guest," giggled Cathy. "It's Ollie the Octopus!"

"I need a plate for each of my eight arms," laughed Ollie as he put a delicious cake onto each plate.

Mike The Mixer

Mike the mixer was brand new. His orange paintwork gleamed, his mixer was spotless, even his tyres were perfectly clean.

It was Mike the mixer's first day out and he was longing to get dirty. "I hope lots of people will want cement," he said to himself, as he drove along the road to find some work.

He hadn't travelled very far before he came to some major roadworks. On the left was a long queue of trucks and lorries waiting to dump their loads.

"Have you brought any stone or tarmac to put on the roads?" shouted the man in charge.

"Nothing at all," replied Mike, "but I'll fetch you a load of cement."

"Don't bother," said the man. "We don't need any here. Now get out of the way!"

So Mike the mixer hurried on until he came to a building site. "This looks promising," he said to himself, as he parked beside a pile of bricks and some sand.

"Can I fetch you a load of cement?" Mike called to a bricklayer building a wall.

"Too late," yelled the man. "We've almost finished for today. Can you move, you're blocking the way?"

Quickly Mike drove on and turned down the next road where he found a man laying a new path in his garden.

When he saw Mike, the man shouted across, "I've just mixed all this concrete myself and now I've got blisters and backache. You should have come an hour ago!"

"Oh dear!" thought Mike as he drove on. "I won't find any work there."

All the next week Mike tried to find something to do, but nobody wanted a load of cement.

Mike was feeling very sorry for himself, so he drove around until he found a quiet street. He gave a deep sigh and switched off his engine.

At that very moment, Mike heard a loud voice right beside him. "You're just what I need. A cement mixer is the answer to all my problems!" A very excited baker was standing next to him, for Mike had parked right outside his shop.

"Today I must bake the tallest birthday cake in the world," the busy baker explained. "I don't have a bowl big enough to mix the cake and my poor arms will ache with all that stirring. Will you help me out?"

Mike the cement mixer was thrilled - a job at last!

The busy baker got to work at once. He loaded butter, sugar, flour and dried fruit into Mike's mixer. Then he tossed in one hundred eggs and a whole box of spices.

Mike started his engine and his mixer began to turn. The busy baker shouted, "Whoa!" when he thought everything was ready. Then Mike tilted his mixer and poured the cake-mix into eleven giant cake tins.

The cakes took hours to bake. When they were ready and had cooled, the baker decorated them with pink sugar icing, while Mike watched through the shop door.

"Who ordered such a giant cake?" Mike asked the baker that night.

"I've no idea!" replied the busy baker, shaking his head. "We shall find out tomorrow."

And find out they did! Next morning the zoo keeper arrived with some of his staff to take the giant cake back with them to the zoo.

"Today is our giraffe's birthday and we wanted a cake as tall as him!"

The baker and Mike were invited to the zoo and asked to join the party.

"Could you stay and work for me and mix cakes instead of cement?" the baker asked Mike.

Mike the cake mixer agreed at once!

The Counting Caterpillar

Some caterpillars like to munch leaves and stalks all day, while others nibble fruit and flowers.

Colin the caterpillar was different. He loved to count!

To begin with, he counted from one to ten. It wasn't long before he could count up to a hundred.

As Colin crawled slowly along he counted the world around him...one bud on a rose, two wings on a wasp, three bugs in a jar, four wings on a dragonfly, five grubs in a peach, six legs on a cricket, seven stripes on a beetle, eight legs on a spider, nine leaves on a plant and ten petals on a daisy.

Colin counted all day long. He counted the insects buzzing around him and the ants as they marched through the long grass.

First thing every morning as Colin was busy counting, a bright red ladybird and her family passed by on their way to the rose garden. Mother ladybird had six black spots, each baby had two.

"Good morning," called Colin counting out loud. "Sixteen spots, twelve feelers, thirty-six legs, have a nice day!"

Then Colin crawled off and spent the rest of that day counting the seeds in a giant sunflower. When all the ladybirds returned later that day,

things did not add up. Colin was puzzled. Quickly he counted fourteen spots, ten feelers, and only thirty legs. Something was wrong!

One young ladybird had been left behind, but was soon found upside-down in a rose petal.

"Everyone should learn to count!" said Mother Ladybird as she thanked Colin. "It's very useful."

"I agree!" nodded Colin wisely. "Tomorrow I shall count up to 1,000!"

The Pumpkin Man

One day in spring Joe the gardener planted some seeds in his vegetable plot. Joe's cat and dog and even his white rabbit lent a hand.

"When the autumn comes," said Joe, "we shall have plenty of pumpkins!"

Joe was absolutely right. At harvest time his garden was full of ripe orange pumpkins of every shape and size.

Joe, his cat and dog and even his white rabbit had never seen so many pumpkins.

"I shall pick the biggest one," said Joe proudly, "and we shall have pumpkin pie every day."

"Ugh!" groaned Joe's cat and dog and even his rabbit, because they hated the stuff!

So all that day Joe baked pumpkin pies. He cooked so many they filled the kitchen, but still he had only used up half his biggest pumpkin.

"Time to eat," shouted Joe, as he cut for the cat and dog, and even the white rabbit, a huge slice of pumpkin pie.

"But we hate pumpkin pie!" cried the cat, the dog and even the rabbit.

"And so do I," agreed Joe, when he took his first bite.

"So what can we do with all these pumpkins?" the four friends shouted together.

It was the white rabbit who thought of the best idea.

"Tomorrow is Halloween," he told the others, "everyone will need lots and lots of pumpkins."

So this is what they did.

The rest of that day, Joe and his cat, dog and rabbit, cut and carved the pumpkins ready for Halloween.

When darkness fell, they put a candle in every pumpkin shell and hung them outside the house and all over the garden.

What a beautiful sight hundreds of golden lanterns made with their bright lights flickering in the darkness.

Very soon a huge crowd gathered outside Joe's house. People saw the glowing pumpkin lamps as they passed, and everyone wanted to buy one to take home.

By midnight all the pumpkins had been sold and everyone was happy.

"I love Halloween," sighed the white rabbit, "but best of all I love the pumpkin lanterns."

"Oh my goodness," gasped Joe to his cat and dog. "I'm afraid we've sold the last one."

So the next day, on Halloween, they had to go out and buy a pumpkin - just for the white rabbit.

The Little Red Helicopter

Right on the edge of a busy airport stood the Little Red Helicopter.
All day long he watched the huge jet planes taking off and landing on the runway, as they carried passengers to far away places.

"It must be wonderful taking people on holiday," sighed the Little Red Helicopter, "but nobody ever notices me!"

Every morning the Little Red Helicopter flew businessmen into the city to work and brought them back to the same place every night.

It was very dull. No-one ever smiled at the Little Red Helicopter or thanked him for a nice flight. His passengers ignored him, they were far too busy to notice the Little Red Helicopter.

Now one morning something different happened. A worried looking gentleman came running towards the Little Red Helicopter.

"Can you take off and land in a a very small place?" the gentleman shouted loudly. "Will you please come to our rescue?"

The Little Red Helicopter was overjoyed. Adventure at last! He agreed at once.

Straight away, the staff from the airport pulled out the Little Red Helicopter's seats and began to fill up the space with sacks and bales of hay. How they scratched and tickled the poor Little Red Helicopter.

The pilot climbed in and started the engine, the blades began to spin and soon they were flying high over the airport.

"We must travel across country and up into the hills!" shouted the pilot above all the noise. "Do you think you can land with such a heavy load?"

"I think I can," whirred the Little Red Helicopter. "I'll do my very best."

When he reached the hills the Little Red Helicopter looked down. There were floods everywhere! The countryside below him was covered with water and the animals had been moved to higher ground,

At last the Little Red Helicopter reached the hillside and landed carefully on a very small space.

Everyone clapped and cheered and shouted, "Well done!" They crowded round the Little Red Helicopter and made him feel like a hero.

The animals hadn't eaten for two whole days. Soon they were tucking into the food that the Little Red Helicopter had brought such a long way.

"You've saved the day," said the pilot with a smile. "Would you like to be a rescue helicopter from now on?"

The Little Red Helicopter lifted right off the ground with pride. The very next day the pilot painted the words 'Rescue Helicopter' in black on his side.

85

The Clowns' Breakfast

Three funny circus clowns lived together in one house. One clown washed the clothes, one clown cooked the meals and the other clown kept the house neat and tidy. Most of the time they got on very well, but there was one thing that they could not agree upon.

Every morning before they went to work at the circus, the three funny clowns would have breakfast together.

They all drank fresh coffee with cream and sugar. They all ate hot toast with butter and jam, but most of all they enjoyed boiled eggs in their very own egg cups.

Each morning the three funny clowns sat round the table listening to their eggs as they bubbled in the pan. After exactly four minutes the eggs were ready...and that was when the trouble began!

"That's my egg, put it down!"

"Mine was white, yours is brown!"

"They're just the same, put my egg back!"

"Don't mix them up, they're sure to crack!"

The three funny clowns could never agree which egg was which. That was a pity because their eggs got cold, their toast was burnt and their coffee tasted terrible.

Breakfast was spoiled every day!

"This is no way for three clowns to behave," said the three friends as they gazed at each other sadly.

Suddenly one of the clowns jumped up. "All this fuss over three boiled eggs," he cried, as he pulled a pencil from a pocket in his big baggy trousers. "I have the answer to our problem!"

He picked up one of the eggs and drew a clown's face on it, exactly like his own. Then the other two clowns did the same.

Now, every morning, each clown draws his own face on his egg before popping it into the pan.

When the eggs are ready there are no more problems, just three happy, hungry clowns.

Sam The Scribbling Snake

One day as Sam the Snake slithered along the floor of the steamy jungle, he found a big box of sharp, shiny pencils.

"Ssssuper," hissed Sam. "What a simply smashing surprise!" With that, he picked up a pencil and began to scribble.

First he scribbled in the sand, then he scribbled on the flowers and leaves. Next he scribbled up and down the tree trunks. He even scribbled all over the animals.

Something had to be done!

"Sam has lots of pencils," said the baby elephant, "we must find him lots of paper to scribble on!"

Before very long, the animals came back with notebooks and pads of every shape and size and sheets and sheets of paper.

"Stupendous!" Sam hissed happily. "I'll start slowly by spelling short sentences. Soon I shall scribble short stories about all my friends in the jungle."

Sam scribbled so many stories that some were made into books and films, and very soon Sam the Scribbling Snake became a Superstar!

The Sound Asleep Pig

Patti the pig could not get up in the morning. The bell on her alarm clock rang loudly at seven o'clock, but Patti didn't hear a thing.

At eight o'clock, the rooster from the farmyard perched on top of her bed and crowed as loud as he could for half an hour. Still Patti the pig did not wake up!

"I'll try too!" said the owl, and he hooted from nine until ten. Then he flew home to sleep for the day.

Will nothing wake Patti the pig?

At eleven o'clock, the old grey donkey stuck his head through her bedroom window. He brayed loudly in Patti's ear, until everybody begged him to stop.

How can Patti the pig sleep through all that noise - will she never wake up?

At twelve o'clock the farmer's wife said, "I know how to wake her up!"

She opened Patti's door and shouted, "Dinner time!" In a flash Patti was awake and ready for her dinner.

Now we all know how to wake Patti the sound asleep pig!

Dolly's Telephone

One morning as Dolly was looking in her mirror she gave a little scream. Her face was covered in spots!

"Oh dear! Oh dear!" said the doctor, shaking his head. "You must stay in bed for a whole week."

"But I don't feel in the least bit ill," wailed Dolly, and she went to bed and sulked.

The other toys tried to cheer her up. They came round to visit her. They brought books and games and flowers and chocolates, which they left outside her bedroom door.

"I shall have no-one to talk to for a whole week!" snapped Dolly, and she pulled the bedclothes over her head.

All the toys felt sorry for Dolly, but they didn't want to go near her just in case they caught the spots too.

"I think I know how to help," piped up a tinkling little voice.

It was the toy telephone. "I will go to visit Dolly this afternoon. She can talk to her friends for an hour and that will cheer her up!"

Dolly was thrilled to see the toy telephone and began to dial straight away. "I have dolly friends all over the world," said Dolly proudly. "Now I can phone every one of them!"

"Oh dear," sighed the toy telephone. "It looks as if I shall be here all week!"

Buzz Builds A Snowman

One winter's day, when the snow lay deep in the garden, William asked his friend, Buzz the Robot, if he would like to make a snowman.

"I don't know how! I don't know how!" whirred Buzz.

"Watch me!" laughed William. "It's very easy!"

So William set to work shovelling the soft snow and piling it up high. He shaped the snow very carefully until he had made a perfect snowman.

"All he needs now is a scarf, some gloves and a hat," smiled William as he stepped back to admire his work. "Now you try Buzz!"

The little robot stared at William's snowman, and all his lights flashed on and off. "Not like that! Not like that!" he cried in his funny robot voice.

He whizzed into the house and came back with a bowl of fruit! This made William howl with laughter.

All of a sudden Buzz whirled his robot arms and there was his snowman made in a flash.

"Looks just like me! Looks just like me!" Buzz giggled, as he pointed to his snowman.

"The bowl of fruit was a great idea," said William. "Only a robot could think of that!"

The Flying Fieldmice

Tim and Tilly Fieldmouse were sitting in a cornfield gazing up at the bright blue sky. As they watched the clouds floating by, Tilly spotted something.

Flying high above them was a helicopter. As it came nearer, Tim spotted something else. "Look!" he squeaked, pointing up into the sky, "someone has jumped out!"

Tim and Tilly Fieldmouse held their breath, then all of a sudden a parachute opened up and a man floated gently to the ground.

"I wish we could ride in a helicopter and go parachuting," said Tilly, with a sigh, "but we're far too small!"

When Tilly looked round Tim was gone. He had scampered up to the top of a hill where a tall sycamore tree grew. Underneath the tree, the ground was covered with sycamore seeds - just like tiny wings.

"Look at me Tilly!" cried Tim, as he jumped into the air. "Have you ever seen a flying fieldmouse before?"

What fun both little mice had. They flew around all afternoon, until they were tired out.

"Let's go flying again tomorrow," laughed Tilly, as the two fieldmice went home to bed.

The Monster On The Moon

There were once two little squirrels who lived high up in an old oak tree.

On dark nights, the thing they liked to do most, was to watch the moon from their bedroom window.

"Is there really a Man in the Moon?" they asked Father Squirrel time after time.

So one night he brought his big, brass telescope up to the squirrels' bedroom. "See for yourself!" smiled Father Squirrel as he pointed the telescope up at the dark night sky.

Both little squirrels stood on their tiptoes and took it in turns to look at the moon through the big brass telescope.

"Can you see the Man in the Moon yet?" joked their Father.

All of a sudden, the two little squirrels let go of the telescope and hid under their bed.

"There's a huge monster on the moon with great big staring eyes!" they shouted with fright.

Father Squirrel leaned out of the bedroom window and started to laugh. "It's only Ollie the Owl perched on a branch. He doesn't look much like the Monster on the Moon to me!"

Goodnight Everybody

Mrs Hedgehog had such a large family it took simply ages for her ten children to get ready for bed.

When all the little hedgehogs had been bathed, they sat together in front of a warm fire with milk and biscuits. The very last thing they did before they went to bed, was brush their teeth and comb their bristly spines. All this took a very long time!

At last, when they were all tucked up in bed and Baby Hedgehog was settled down in his wooden cot, Mrs Hedgehog would say goodnight to every one of her ten children.

Ten children, ten goodnights, what a long job! Then all the children would say goodnight to Mrs Hedgehog, and then say goodnight to each other!

Some nights, they would forget Baby Hedgehog, so they had to begin all over again!

"I shall never get my children to sleep," Mrs Hedgehog would sometimes sigh. However, she usually did, although it was often very late.

One night when all the little hedgehogs were fast asleep, Oswald Owl flew into a tree nearby and began to hoot very loudly. All the little hedgehogs woke up at once, got out of their beds and began to play.

"My goodness," exclaimed Mrs Hedgehog when she heard the noise, "whatever shall I do?"

Poor Mrs Hedgehog. This started to happen every night as soon as the ten young hedgehogs fell fast asleep.

"If I knew what time the children went to bed," hooted Oswald, "I could go and hoot in some other part of the wood!"

This gave Mrs Hedgehog an idea. She searched in one of her cupboards and found a large watch.

So, the very next night, she gave it to Oswald the Owl. "You can hoot up to eight o'clock, not a minute longer!"

Oswald was very pleased indeed with his new watch. He hooted every night on a tree nearby while the hedgehog children got ready for bed. They all said goodnight to each other and settled down. Oswald then looked at his watch, hooted goodnight, then flew away.

"Goodnight everybody, goodnight!"

Baby Squirrel's Rescue

One warm summer's evening all the little squirrels were in their bedroom at the top of an oak tree in Forest Town. Although it was past their bedtime, they were all still wide awake.

"I can't go to sleep!" cried Baby Squirrel, as he bounced up and down on his bed. "It's still light and I want to play!"

"Ssshh!!" whispered the others. "Don't make so much noise or Mother will hear you, then we'll all be in trouble!"

"See if I care," Baby Squirrel giggled and bounced up and down even more.

When the other squirrels saw their young brother having so much fun, they decided to join in too. Very soon they were all jumping up and down on the bed and making a dreadful noise.

"Look at me," cried Baby Squirrel, "I can jump higher than any of you!"

All of a sudden, he bounced up into the air, through the open window and landed right on the top branch of the tallest tree in Forest Town. All the little squirrels rushed over to the window.

"Help! Help!" yelled Baby Squirrel as he swung to and fro. "Somebody get me down!"

Just at that very moment, Mother Squirrel burst in through the bedroom door. She had heard all the noise and came to find out what was going on. When she looked out of the window and saw her baby hanging onto the topmost branch of the tallest tree in Forest Town, she could hardly believe her eyes.

"How did you get up there?" she cried in surprise. "Come back in here this minute!" Poor Baby Squirrel was too frightened to reply.

"I can't reach up there!" Mother Squirrel called as she looked up into the branches. "I must send for the Forest Town Fire Brigade."

When the firemen arrived, they looked up into the tall tree and shook

their heads. "Our ladders aren't long enough to reach him," said the Forest Town Fire Chief. "He'll have to jump!"

"Jump?!" screamed Mother Squirrel with fright. All the little squirrels began to cry.

"Don't worry one bit," smiled the Fire Chief as the team of firemen held open a very big safety sheet.

Now when Baby Squirrel looked down into the safety sheet far below, he wasn't a bit afraid. "I'll pretend I'm bouncing on my bed," he called to the firemen. "Watch out, here I come!"

Baby Squirrel flew through the air and landed in the safety sheet quite unharmed.

"That was marvellous!" squealed Baby Squirrel with delight. "Can I do it again?"

"Certainly not!" snapped his mother. "Off to bed with you and no more bouncing up and down."

That night the little squirrels dreamt they were firemen. Baby Squirrel, meanwhile, was dreaming of flying through the air on a trapeze at the circus!

Professor Smart's New Invention

Jack lived next door to Professor Smart. One night, when the Professor's lights were on very late, Jack guessed he would be inventing something.

"Come and look at my new car!" the Professor shouted to Jack over the garden fence the next morning.

But Jack didn't have to go anywhere because the car came to him! It drove up one side of the fence, across the top and down the other side.

"It's a remote controlled car," Jack gasped, "what a beauty!"

The little blue car shot across the flowerbeds, straight through the greenhouse and out the other side. Then it climbed up the garden step and through the stone fountain.

"I'd better catch it before it wrecks Dad's prize dahlias!" cried Jack.

The little remote controlled car certainly had caused havoc.

"Help Jack!" cried the Professor. "Catch it if you can!"

As he ran past the garden shed, Jack had a bright idea. He grabbed his dad's large fishing net and scooped up the car in a moment.

"Thank goodness!" the Professor sighed with relief. "The car works perfectly, but I haven't invented a way to stop it yet!"

"I think you'd better do that right away," laughed Jack, as he handed back the car, "before it does any more damage!"

Smile, It's A Crocodile

There once was a very friendly crocodile. He loved meeting people, talking and going out to parties.

Sad to say, he didn't meet many people, so he hardly ever talked to anyone, and he never got asked to parties! Now why do you think that was?

The crocodile was so nice and friendly that he smiled all the time. And when he smiled, he showed his teeth - rows and rows of sharp pointed teeth that sparkled in the sun.

If you smiled at a crocodile and he smiled back, would you go up and shake his hand just to be friendly?

Oh no, you'd run away as fast as you could! And this, unfortunately, was just what happened. Every single time the crocodile smiled, people would run away, they never smiled back.

One day, the poor crocodile was so lonely, he took a walk into town. He smiled nicely at everyone he met. He even grinned at every single person in a bus queue, but not one of them

smiled back. Instead, they fled in all directions.

"Oh dear!" exclaimed the crocodile. "They've missed their bus!"

Then all alone, he walked into a store and smiled politely at the assistants. Most of them dived behind the counter and one of them climbed on top of the shelves!

"Oh dear!" said the crocodile, looking around. "Where have all the customers gone?"

Feeling rather glum, he walked a little further down the street. He hadn't gone very far before a man in a white coat came running towards him.

"I'll try to be nice just once more," said the crocodile, grinning widely and showing every one of his sharp pointed teeth.

The man didn't just smile back, he threw his arms around the crocodile and did a little dance in the middle of the street.

"What a beautiful smile!" cried the man in delight. "I am a dentist and you must have the best set of teeth I have ever seen!"

The crocodile went quite red.

"Please come and be my new model and assistant!" begged the dentist. "You can show everyone how to brush their teeth properly, then they'll have a sparkling smile just like yours!"

Of course, the crocodile said yes. Soon, people came flooding to the dentist, just to see a crocodile brushing his teeth.

Now, everyone smiles at the crocodile and he smiles back proudly, his rows and rows of teeth sparkling even more with all that brushing!

Lucy, The Long-legged Goose

It was Halloween and everyone in the farmyard was getting very excited. The animals were looking forward to a very special party that night, but most of all they were looking forward to dressing up.

"I'm going as a Red Indian!" grunted the pig.

"Then I'll be a cowboy!" giggled the goat.

"And what will you be?" the farmer asked Lucy, the long-legged goose.

"It's a secret!" honked Lucy as she scurried across the farmyard. Now Lucy the goose had been planning her costume for weeks and wanted it to be a great surprise.

Late that night, when the moon was full and everyone was at the party, a dark shadow flitted across the sky.

"A witch!" someone gasped. Everyone looked up. There, high above the trees, was a witch on a broomstick circling round ready to swoop down on the animals in the farmyard.

"It's a real witch!" someone else cried. They all ran to hide, quite scared out of their wits.

The witch's broomstick landed in the middle of the farmyard with a thump. One by one the animals peered from their hiding places and then began to laugh.

"It's not a witch at all!" they roared.

"It's Lucy the long-legged goose! I'd know those bright yellow legs anywhere!" chuckled the farmer.

108

Barney Knows Best!

Lisa had a brand new winter outfit. "What great clothes," said Lisa proudly. "I shall never take them off!"

Her little dog, Barney, sniggered because he knew that she would have to soon enough!

"I shall wear my new outfit in the rain, in the snow and when the cold wind blows. I shall never ever take it off!"

Her little dog, Barney, smiled to himself and gazed up into the sky.

The sun came out from behind a cloud and soon it felt very warm.

"Phew!" gasped Lisa. "I'll have to take off this outfit and find a cooler one!"

Her little dog, Barney, chuckled to himself, "I just knew she would!"

Tibby Goes To Sleep

Philip's cat, Tibby, sleeps anywhere - in a cardboard box or the back of a chair! She sleeps in the strangest of places all over the house, and no-one can find her when it's time to go out.

When the family get up in the morning, if nobody is looking, she will creep into someone's warm bed and stay there all morning!

Philip is getting ready for his first day at a new school. He would like to say goodbye to Tibby, but as usual, she is nowhere to be found.

Perhaps Philip won't miss Tibby at school as much as he thinks!

Patti's Portrait

Patti the pig was wandering through the meadow one fine, summer morning. She paused for a minute to smell the flowers and gaze up into the clear, blue sky.

"What a lovely morning," she sighed, "and what beautiful, beautiful flowers."

"And what a beautiful pig!" said a voice from behind.

Patti turned round, rather startled. There, sitting in the long grass, was an artist painting a picture.

"I've never seen a more beautiful pig," the artist went on, "I simply must paint your picture!"

"How wonderful," squealed Patti, very thrilled. "But I've absolutely nothing to wear!" And before the artist could stop her, she trotted away at top speed.

Very soon, Patti the pig returned to the farm and quietly tiptoed into the farmhouse. No-one was in, so she turned upstairs. She searched inside cupboards and drawers until she found a hat and a dress, a necklace and some shoes that belonged to the farmer's wife.

"Perfect!" Patti sighed as she gazed in the mirror. "I really am the most beautiful pig!"

When the artist saw Patti, he shook his head. "Where is that beautiful pig that I met in the meadow this morning?"

"I'm here!" squealed Patti. "I've dressed up for the picture!"

"No need," replied the artist, "you were quite exquisite before!"

So, Patti carefully folded up the farmer's wife's clothes, then stood very still in the meadow sniffing the flowers.

When the artist had finished his painting, he hung it in an art gallery. One day he took Patti along to see for herself what a very beautiful picture she made!

The Shy Kangaroo

"It's hard to make friends when you're shy. But it's worth it, so give it a try..." the shy little kangaroo's mother told him every day. But the little kangaroo was far too shy to jump out of his mother's pouch, instead he just peeped over the top.

One day he almost made it, but a noisy cockatoo screeched, "How are you?" so loudly in his ear, that he jumped back in his mother's pouch and would not come out again.

"You're missing all the fun," whispered his mother. "Come out and find a friend!"

Now a koala who lived in the trees above could see the little kangaroo hiding inside his mother's pouch, and he really did want to be his friend.

He thought for a long time and at last came up with an idea he thought might work. He came down from the trees, stood in front of Mother Kangaroo and stared at the ground.

The koala stayed in exactly the same spot all morning, just staring down.

The shy little kangaroo watched him for hours, his head just peeping out of his mother's pouch. At last, he simply had to find out what the koala was staring at.

All at once he jumped out of the pouch and landed right in front of the koala.

"Will you be my friend?" asked the koala as he hugged the little kangaroo.

"If you will tell me what you are looking at on the ground," whispered the little kangaroo.

"Nothing at all!" giggled the koala, "but it made you come out of your mother's pouch to find out. Now you're not shy any more!"

Koala Keeps Up

Kangaroo and Koala were the very best of friends and spent lots of time together. They liked to go to the country, they liked to visit the town, and anywhere else that took their fancy...but there was just one problem!

Kangaroo could travel very quickly hopping along at speed, but poor Koala couldn't keep up.

"Don't leave me behind!" he puffed. "I can't run very fast, my legs are too short!"

Kangaroo thought for a while. "I know just the thing!" he laughed. "Now you'll never get left behind!"

Kangaroo Takes Off!

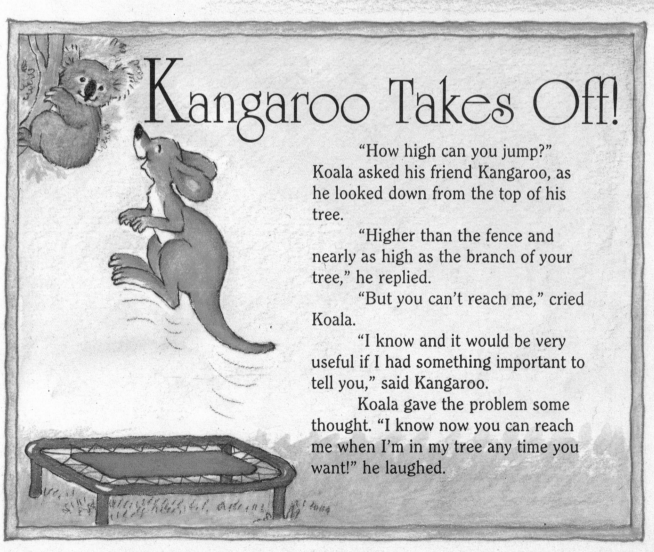

"How high can you jump?" Koala asked his friend Kangaroo, as he looked down from the top of his tree.

"Higher than the fence and nearly as high as the branch of your tree," he replied.

"But you can't reach me," cried Koala.

"I know and it would be very useful if I had something important to tell you," said Kangaroo.

Koala gave the problem some thought. "I know now you can reach me when I'm in my tree any time you want!" he laughed.

The Blue Engine's Big Surprise

One day a visitor came to look around the huge sheds at the railway station where the trains were kept.

"I am looking for a special engine," he told the stationmaster. "I need an engine that is not too big and not too small. I need an engine that is strong enough to pull lots of wagons a long way!"

"The Little Blue Engine over there is just what you want," said the stationmaster, "but I'm afraid he is a little rusty and some of his wagons are falling to pieces!"

"Don't worry one bit!" the visitor told the stationmaster. "I shall take care of everything!"

The Little Blue Engine was very pleased. He had been standing in the railway station shed for a long time with no-one to talk to and nothing to do.

The very next morning, a gang of people arrived. They scrubbed and rubbed and polished the Little Blue Engine's paint work and cleaned all the brass until it sparkled and shone. Then they set to work mending and

painting all the wagons and carriages. The Little Blue Engine had never looked so smart.

'I wonder when the passengers will arrive and where I be taking them,' thought the Engine. It was all very exciting!

He didn't have to wait long to find out. Very soon the driver climbed aboard and the Little Blue Engine pulled out of the shed and whistled goodbye to the other trains left behind.

As he pulled into the station, he heard the announcer saying, "The train arriving at platform one is the new circus train to take the Big Top Circus anywhere it wants to go. Goodbye Little Blue Engine and good luck!"

Laura's New Shoes

Laura loved new shoes. She loved going to the shoe shop and taking ages to choose her favourite pair. Then she loved walking home in her new shoes, carrying her old ones back in a cardboard box.

One day her mother said, "Laura, the toes of your shoes are scuffed and the heels look a little worn. Put on your coat and we'll go to the shop to choose some new ones!"

The shoe shop was empty, so Laura could take her time to look around at all the new styles and different colours.

At last her mother said, "Laura, you have had lots of time to choose, which pair would you like?"

Laura sighed. She loved the shiny patent leather ones with the ankle straps and silver buckles. She thought the pink shoes decorated with tiny hearts and fastened with pearl buttons were simply wonderful. But most of all she really wanted the red and yellow shoes with fancy laces.

"Laura," said her mother. "Have you made up your mind?"

Laura took a deep breath and pointed to some dull brown slip-on shoes hidden at the bottom of the racks.

"I'll have that pair," whispered Laura, "and I would like to leave my old shoes on and carry the new ones home in the box!"

Inside the box was a doll. Not an ordinary doll, but a doll with laces and buttons and bows, even zips, all over her clothes.

"If you practise on this special doll, you'll soon learn to fasten anything!"

And that is exactly what Laura did. So, the next time she went shopping to buy shoes, Laura chose just what she really wanted!

The rest of that day, Laura was very quiet. She took her new shoes upstairs and put them in her wardrobe. She didn't even try them on, but kept them shut away in the cardboard box.

"Laura," said her mother as she put her to bed that night, "why did you choose such a dull pair of shoes?"

Poor Laura looked miserable. "All the nicest shoes in the shop had buckles, bows or buttons, and I can't fasten any of those!"

How Laura's mother laughed. "Is that all?" she said. "I know an easy way to learn, but you will have to wait until tomorrow to find out!"

Early next morning, Laura's mother went to the shops, but she didn't take Laura. When she returned she was carrying a parcel in fancy wrapping paper.

"Is it a present for me?" asked Laura eagerly.

"Open it and see," replied her mother.

Evangeline Sets Sail

One day Evangeline the china doll and her friends went to the pond for a picnic. As they sat on the grass eating their lunch, they watched the boats sailing across the boating lake.

"I would like to go for a sail," said Evangeline as she reached for the last chocolate biscuit.

The sailor doll and the others had a wonderful time skimming across the water all afternoon. As for Evangeline, she stayed in the same spot for hours.

"Do you need any help?" the sailor doll shouted as he sped by.

"That's a good idea!" said the sailor doll jumping up quickly. "We'll hire a boat right away!"

"I want that one with the big striped sail!" shouted Evangeline as the sailor doll crossed the grass. "You others can share the small boat!"

"Have you ever sailed before, Evangeline?" asked the blue rabbit.

"Lots of times!" snapped Evangeline as she floated away in the biggest boat.

"None at all!" Evangeline yelled back tossing her head in the air.

All of a sudden, she overbalanced and fell overboard and her boat floated away to the other side of the lake.

"Help! Help!" Evangeline screamed as she thrashed about in the water. "It's very cold and my curls are getting wet! Get me out at once!"

"I thought you were a good sailor!" laughed the sailor doll as he steered his boat towards her. The others were giggling too!

"Stop laughing at once!" screamed Evangeline. "If you don't rescue me, I shall drown!"

This made her friends laugh so much that they almost upset their boat. That part of the lake was very shallow and everyone knew that if Evangeline stood up, she would be quite safe.

"You're in no danger at all!" smiled the sailor doll. And when Evangeline stopped splashing about and stood up, the water came just above her knees. The sailor doll helped Evangeline into the boat with all the others.

"Why did you make such a fuss?" asked the blue rabbit.

"How was I to know that the water wasn't deep?" cried Evangeline dripping wet. "You see, I can't swim!"

Everyone gasped. "You can't swim?" they all chorused. "Then you must learn straight away!"

Now, how Evangeline learnt to swim is another story...

Bill's New Job

Once upon a time there was a very nice man named Bill. He worked in an office, but found his job very tiresome.

"Oh dear!" sighed Bill, at the end of a very long dull week, "I really must look for another job, one a bit more exciting!"

So, that very day, he put away his pens, said goodbye to everybody in the office and left.

"What job shall I do now?" Bill asked himself, as he walked home. "Shall I be a farmer, or a baker, or a bus driver, or a bricklayer?" Bill wondered if he needed special training for these jobs. Suddenly, he thought of a marvellous idea, "I'll be a burglar! - that's sure to be different!"

So that day, Bill went to the library and took out a book called *How To Be A Successful Burglar*.

'You will need soft shoes to walk on tiptoe, a mask to disguise your face, a powerful torch to use on pitch-black nights, a rope ladder to climb in and out of tall buildings...' the book said, '...and a big sack to carry the loot.'

"Oh dear me," gasped Bill. "I hate heights and I'm afraid of the dark, but I do want to be a burglar." He thought for a while, "I know I'll go out in the daytime!"

The very next morning, Bill took some money out of his bank account and bought all the things he needed to be a real burglar.

The afternoon was bright and sunny. "What a lovely day for my very first burglary," said Bill, so straight away he set off down the road with his mask on his face and a huge sack slung over his shoulder.

As Bill walked through the town, people came out of the banks and shops to say hello to their friend as he passed by. "How can I be a burglar with this crowd behind me?" said Bill, rather surprised.

At last, they reached the town hall and the Mayor himself came out to greet Bill. "What a wonderful costume!" laughed the Mayor as he handed Bill an enormous silver cup. "You have just won first prize in this afternoon's fancy dress competition! Well done!"

Everybody cheered, but Bill looked a bit glum. "I'll never make a burglar!" he sighed. "Everyone has recognised me and now I don't have a job!"

Poor Bill took off his burglar's mask and sat down on the steps of the town hall.

"Would you like a job working for me?" asked the Mayor, who saw how downhearted Bill looked. "I need someone to drive my long black car and look after my golden regalia!"

Bill agreed at once. He put on his brand new chauffeur's uniform and while no-one was looking, threw the burglar's outfit into the nearest dustbin!

Let's Go On Holiday

Very early one morning, the zoo keeper put a notice on the gates of the zoo which read, *Closed For Two Weeks Holiday.*

The animals were most surprised and wondered what to do.

"We need a holiday," said the keeper, "but don't worry, someone will come to look after you."

The animals looked around in dismay. "But we need a holiday too," they muttered amongst themselves.

There and then, some of the animals agreed to pack their bags, walk through the zoo gates and go to the seaside.

They hadn't gone very far before some of the little ones began to feel tired. "Are we near yet?" asked the smallest monkey, "it's a long way to the seaside and my feet hurt already."

So everyone sat down for a rest. Just then, around the corner came Ellie Elephant. "Jump on my back and I will take you all to the seaside. I'll be your taxi and we'll be there in next to no time!"

"Three cheers for Ellie!" the animals cried, "and three cheers for our holiday!"

Evangeline's Tea Party

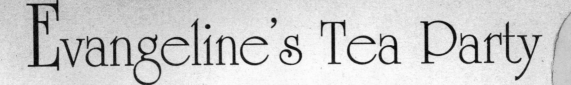

One day Evangeline the china doll thought she would give a tea party. So right away, she made lots of tiny iced buns and plenty of dainty sandwiches. She made a jug of lemonade and one of orange, then put them in the refrigerator to cool.

Next she set out all the garden furniture and last of all put up her huge yellow sun umbrella, just to keep the hot sun from spoiling the tiny cakes and wafer thin sandwiches.

"Oh dear!" sighed all her neighbours. "Evangeline is giving one of her tea parties. They're so very dull. Everybody has to be on their best behaviour and sit still all afternoon!"

"Hurry up everyone!" called Evangeline, in her loudest voice. "Sit up straight and don't put your elbows on the table!" Evangeline could be very bossy at times.

All of a sudden, a strong gust of wind blew the yellow sun umbrella up into the air. It went flying over the roof-tops, through the park and into the field beyond.

Poor Evangeline jumped up and down in temper. "My tea party is ruined!" she screamed. "Go after my umbrella at once."

So all her friends ran across the field to try and catch up with Evangeline's yellow sun umbrella.

"Isn't this fun?" gasped the sailor doll, quite out of breath. "Evangeline's tea party isn't dull after all!"

At last they caught up with the yellow sun umbrella - and where do you think it was? Upside down in Farmer Jones' duck pond!

"Get it out at once!" screamed Evangeline, having one of her tantrums. "It will get all wet and muddy!"

"There, there, young lady," said Farmer Jones, trying not to laugh. "My ducks will get it out for you."

"My tea party is ruined!" sobbed poor Evangeline. "My cakes will have melted in the hot sun and the sandwiches will be all curly at the edges!"

By the time the ducks had floated the yellow sun umbrella to the edge of the pond, everyone was feeling very hungry.

"Come and have tea with us," suggested the farmer's wife with a wink, "but I'm afraid it won't be dainty cakes and tiny sandwiches!"

Soon everyone was tucking in to a huge spread of bread and cheese, pies and pastries. They all enjoyed a wonderful farmhouse tea, especially Evangeline, who surprised everyone by eating far more than anyone else!

The Golden Egg

There was once a little brown hen who laid eggs on a nest of straw in a corner of the farmyard. They were big brown eggs and the farmer's wife always collected them very carefully in her basket.

Now the little brown hen was not at all content with sitting on her nest of straw laying brown eggs.

"I wish I could lay golden eggs!" she sighed, "or just one would do, then I would be happy!"

Some of the other hens scratching in the farmyard overheard what the little brown hen had said and they began to cluck. "She wants to lay golden eggs!" they said. "Brown eggs aren't good enough for her!"

The hens made so much noise that all the animals in the farmyard heard. This made the poor little brown hen feel rather silly as she sat on her nest laying eggs for breakfast.

Now when the farmer's wife found out about the little brown hen's wish, she smiled to herself, for she knew exactly what to do.

As it was springtime and very near to Easter, everyone was looking forward to brightly coloured eggs. So, the farmer's wife took a basket of big brown eggs and painted and decorated them in wonderful patterns, except for the biggest brown egg, which she sprayed with shiny gold paint.

Later, when she went to collect the eggs, she slipped the golden egg underneath the little brown hen.

After a while, when the little brown hen hopped off her nest, she turned and saw the glittering golden egg.

She made such a noise that everyone in the farmyard came rushing over. "My wish has been granted," she clucked. "I have laid a golden egg at last, now I will be happy!"

The little brown hen asked the farmer's wife to place her wonderful golden egg in a window that overlooked the farmyard so that she could look at it whenever she wanted...and there it is to this day!

Lemon Is Locked Out

Joe and Kate had a new puppy. They named him Lemon because his fur was of the palest yellow.

Now, like all puppies, Lemon was very mischievous and very inquisitive. He liked to explore cardboard boxes and kitchen cupboards, but best of all he liked to play hide and seek near the fence at the bottom of the garden.

One day, Lemon found a loose board in the fence. Being an inquisitive little puppy, he poked his nose into the space and wriggled through to the street. Then away he went to explore the world outside. When he came back he couldn't find the loose board at all.

Someone had mended the hole in the fence and he was shut out. Lemon sat down and began to howl as loud as he could.

Joe and Kate heard him and came running to the fence. "You silly puppy!" they called. "Dad has mended the fence, but look, the garden gate is wide open!"

Lemon jumped up at once and wagging his stumpy little tail, he trotted in for tea!

Hoot's Big Secret

Hoot the tugboat worked in a busy harbour. All day, Hoot and the other tugboats guided the large ships along. Sometimes, they helped them stop in exactly the right place alongside the quay. Other times, the tugboats towed long lines of barges behind them from one part of the dock to the other, so that they could unload their cargos.

Now Hoot was the smallest of all the tugboats, but he was the strongest. He could pull the biggest of ships along by himself and needed no help from the other tugboats at all!

Now one day, the largest ship ever to come into the harbour was waiting outside. It was the tugboat's job to guide the great ship through the deepest water and enter the narrow harbour gates.

"It's far too big for us to move!" said one tugboat, as he stared up at the ship towering above him.

Then Hoot came racing across the harbour! All on his very own, he pulled the ship forward and it sailed though the gates with no bother at all.

"Hurray for Hoot!" the tugboats cheered. The big ship blew its great siren and all the boats in the harbour joined in. What a noise!

'How can a tiny tugboat pull such a great ship?' everyone wondered. Hoot knew the answer and so do you - but keep it a secret won't you!

Holly's Hide-out

Holly Hare hated gardening, it was hard work and far too messy! Sometimes, when the weather was warm, Holly sat in the flower garden and sunbathed, but she never set foot in the vegetable plot, just in case she might be asked to do something.

One day, as she was sitting outside reading, Holly suddenly felt very hungry. "I think, just this once, I shall stroll over to the vegetable plot and see what I can find!"

As there was no-one in sight, she picked a great armful of crisp lettuces, a big bunch of juicy carrots and an enormous cauliflower.

"I shall eat them all myself," giggled Holly. "I'll hide inside this little house where no-one will see me!"

Once inside, Holly quietly closed the door and began munching straight away.

As she tucked into her second carrot, Holly felt that someone was watching her. Slowly, she turned round and what do you think she saw? Every one of the Hare family watching her from behind the glass.

How the young hares laughed and how Holly blushed, especially when Father Hare gave her a spade and made her dig over the vegetable plot as a punishment for being so greedy!

Barnaby Goes Fishing

When Barnaby Bear felt like a lazy day, he always went fishing in Silver Lake.

He had his own special place by the lake shore and after he had been fishing for a while, he usually dozed off to sleep.

But today was different! "I feel full of energy this morning," said Barnaby, as he jogged along the shore, "the sun is hot and Silver Lake looks so inviting, I think I shall go for a swim!"

So Barnaby Bear took off his clothes and hung them carefully on a bush. Then he plunged into the clear waters of Silver Lake. He splashed around for over an hour until he began to feel very hungry.

"I'll get dried and dressed as quick as I can!" said Barnaby, thinking of the delicious food packed inside his picnic basket.

He stepped out of the water, shook his thick wet fur and looked around. "Where are my clothes?" he gasped. "I'm sure I left them on that bush over there!"

But the bush was quite empty, not so much as a sock in sight!

What had happened was, when Barnaby Bear hung up his clothes earlier, he hadn't noticed a moose in the bushes nibbling away. By accident Barnaby's clothes had got hooked upon the moose's antlers.

Poor old Barnaby, he'll probably have to go home wearing the picnic basket!

Evangeline Buys A Car

One day, Evangeline the china doll wanted to go shopping. "Bother!" she snapped as she looked out of the door, "it's raining and I shall get wet!"

"Never mind, I shall take you in my car!" It was the clown doll who lived next door.

"Don't bother!" said Evangeline, rather rudely. "Your car looks so silly. The doors drop off and the bonnet flies open, and people laugh when you drive down the street!"

The clown doll looked rather sad. He was very fond of Evangeline, although she was often horrid to him.

"I could walk to the shops with you and shelter you from the rain with my giant umbrella," said the clown doll very kindly.

"Alright," snapped Evangeline, "it's better than nothing!"

As the clown doll and Evangeline were walking towards town, they passed a car showroom.

"I've just had a wonderful idea!" shrieked Evangeline, clapping her hands. "I'll go inside and buy a brand new car. You can help me choose clown doll!"

So, Evangeline marched into the showroom and in her loudest voice said, "I'll have the biggest car you have!"

The salesman looked very pleased and showed her the biggest and most expensive model in the showroom.

"I'll take it," said Evangeline very grandly.

"But Evangeline..." whispered the clown doll. "It won't..."

"Silence!" snapped Evangeline. "Drive this model home at once!"

As he drove home, the poor clown doll tried to speak, but Evangeline would not listen to a single word.

"I'm so proud of my flashy new car," sighed Evangeline, as she waved grandly to people they passed in the street.

At last, they reached home. "Park it in my garage," Evangeline ordered the clown doll with a wave of her hand.

"I can't do that!" replied the clown doll as he parked the car in the street outside. "Your new car is far too big for your garage, it's even too wide to go through your gate!"

"Oh dear me!" cried Evangeline, looking a bit ashamed. "I should have listened to you. You'll have to take my lovely car back."

"Why can't you take it back yourself?" asked the clown doll.

"Because I don't know how to drive!" whispered Evangeline, almost in tears.

How the clown doll laughed. "What a silly doll you are Evangeline! Before you buy another car, I will teach you to drive. Then we will choose one that will fit into your garage!"

Evangeline told the clown doll that she was sorry and learnt to drive in his funny circus car - even though parts did fall off sometimes!

Simon Takes Flight!

Once upon a time, there was a snail called Simon. All day long he was content just crawling slowly along the garden path. Sometimes, just for a change, he would crawl slowly up the garden wall - but this would take nearly all morning! Then, in the afternoon, he would slowly crawl down again!

Now Simon the snail was very happy with his way of life, but others around criticised.

All the birds and the bees, the mosquitoes, moths and insects that flew above him said, "Simon, you are so dull. You can't fly and you never see anything of the world but the garden wall and the path!"

Simon thought for a while, then he had to agree. "I wish I had wings and could see the world over the garden wall!"

Poor Simon felt so sad as he crawled away, he didn't even bother to look where he was going.

All of a sudden, the wind began to blow and Simon the snail was lifted up high above the garden. Higher and higher he flew until he was over the tops of the trees, almost as high as the clouds.

When Simon looked down in amazement, he could see fields and towns, mountains and rivers - he even glimpsed the bright blue sea. It was marvellous!

This is what had happened. A boy in the garden was flying his kite and as Simon crawled along, he landed on the tail and had been blown with the kite into the air.

"I can't wait to tell the others all about my adventure!" chuckled Simon, the flying snail, as he crawled slowly back down the garden path.

The Magical Snowmen

One wintery night an icy wind started to blow, then softly and silently, snow began to fall. As children in the Square awoke and looked out of their windows, everything was white. The gardens, the roads and the paths were all covered with a thick blanket of powdery, white snow.

As if by magic, all the front doors in the Square seemed to burst open at once! Out came children dressed in warm scarves, hats and boots all shrieking with delight. Dogs were rolling and barking in the snow, cats were howling to be let back inside with damp paws and wet whiskers.

The grown-ups however, were clearing up with every brush and shovel they could find. "Snow is such a nuisance!" they grumbled.

"Isn't it wonderful!" yelled the children.

All that day, the children played outside. They had the biggest snowball fight ever seen in the Square, and before darkness fell, each had built a snowman by their front gate.

That night, the children were so tired, they went to bed early and fell asleep straight away.

Now it may have been the town hall clock striking midnight that woke up all the children, or it may have been the moon shining bright on the snow covered Square, but one by one every single boy and girl woke up, got out of bed and looked out of the window. You'll never guess what they saw!

Down in the Square below, their snowmen were having a wonderful time. Some were shaking hands and hugging one another, some were dancing up and down or sliding on the slippery paths. How the children stared when their snowmen all joined in a splendid snowball fight in the moonlight!

The fun went on until the moon went behind a cloud and the Square was dark. Then one by one, the tired children slipped back into their warm beds and fell fast asleep.

Next morning, when the children woke up, they all rushed over to their windows, drew back the curtains and looked into the Square.

There they saw the snowmen standing perfectly still by each front gate. Perhaps it had been a dream after all...but if the children had looked even more closely that snowy winter's morning, they may have noticed that all their snowmen had in fact changed places in the night!

Rescue On The Bridge

It had seemed a very long week for the Yellow Rescue Helicopter. He had made no rescues at all! Not one single person had floated out of their depth at sea on an air bed. No-one had been stranded on the rocks as the tide came in, and nobody had fallen down the cliffs and needed help.

The Yellow Rescue Helicopter was bored! "I've not moved from this spot for a whole week," he moaned. "I will soon forget how to fly and my blades might get rusty!"

Then all of a sudden the emergency bell rang, the sirens howled and the rescue pilot came running across the airfield.

He started the blades up at once and shouted above the noise, "We're needed urgently! Fly as fast as you can to the bridge over the bay!"

The Yellow Rescue Helicopter took off at once and was soon swooping low over the water. The pilot guided him under the bridge, then swept up over the top.

As he gazed below, the Yellow Rescue Helicopter could see no-one in the water and no boats in trouble at all.

"Look down there," shouted the pilot, "the bridge is blocked!"

Two gigantic lorries crossing the bridge had broken down. No traffic could cross and the lorries were far too big to be towed away.

"Can you fly close to the bridge, just above one the lorries?" yelled the pilot.

It was very difficult for the Yellow Rescue Helicopter to hover over one spot. The pilot threw out an anchor on a wire which caught onto the back of the lorry.

Very, very carefully, the Yellow Rescue Helicopter flew backwards and dragged the lorry clear of the bridge.

The pilot cheered. "Well done! Now we must fly back and move the other one too!"

The second lorry was even bigger. It took every bit of the Yellow Rescue Helicopter's power to pull the lorry across, but at last they reached the end of the bridge.

Very soon the traffic was speeding across once again. All the drivers honked their horns to thank the Yellow Rescue Helicopter and the pilot as they drove past.

"Well done!" said the pilot, as he flew back to base. "I think that's enough excitement for today." And the Yellow Rescue Helicopter agreed!

Leonard, The Bold, Brave Lion

"I'm bold, brave and fearless!" shouted Leonard the lion to all of his friends.

"Of course you are," they sighed because they had all heard Leonard boasting many times before.

One day when they were walking in the forest listening to Leonard boasting as usual, they turned a corner and saw a castle. On the gate outside was a notice that read, *One Castle For Sale*.

"That's just the right place for me!" cried Leonard. "A bold, brave and fearless lion should live in a castle, then I will be King of the Castle!"

"It looks a bit spooky to me," said one of his friends. "Won't you be frightened when darkness comes?"

"Don't be ridiculous!" snapped Leonard. "I am a bold, brave and fearless lion!"

So Leonard bought the castle at once and moved in the very next day. All his friends came round to help. It was very hard work moving Leonard's heavy furniture up the winding stone staircase.

At last, everything was unpacked and in place. Leonard's friends waved goodbye and set off for home.

Now, the rest of that day Leonard was so busy marching around shouting, "I'm the King of the Castle!" that he forgot to look where the light switches were. So that night, when it grew dark he couldn't find his way!

143

He crept round the room trying to find the door, then he groped along the wall feeling for the light switch.

"Oh dear," Leonard trembled. "It's very spooky all alone in the dark."

Then all at once a door creaked open and something brushed across Leonard's nose.

"It's a ghost!" he screamed. "Perhaps it's a bat, or a witch, or a skeleton or maybe it's a lion-eating monster!"

Poor Leonard began to shake and quiver and quake all over from head to toe. Then he stretched out a paw and touched something slimey, he turned round and felt something nudge against him.

"Help! Help!" cried Leonard, in a squeaky voice. "I wish I really was bold, brave and fearless."

Just then the door opened and the light was switched on, and there stood all Leonard's friends.

"Why are you standing in the dark?" asked one.

"Haven't you noticed our special surprise?" said another.

Leonard looked around the room. The table was set for a party, with a big iced cake and lots of party food.

"I thought the room was full of monsters and ghosts," whispered Leonard, still trembling.

"Here are your ghosts!" said one friend, and he pointed to the streamers and balloons that had brushed Leonard's nose and nudged him in the dark.

"And here is your slimey monster!" laughed another, as he stuck a spoon in a big jelly on the table.

"We got the party ready this afternoon," the friends explained. "Then we came back tonight to join in the fun."

Leonard looked very relieved. "I am a silly lion," he grinned. "I've had such a fright and it's all my own fault!"

His friends gathered round to listen. "I'm not really a bold, brave, fearless lion at all," he said, and everybody smiled. "This castle is so big, I would like you all to come and live here with me."

All his friends thought that this was a wonderful idea and agreed at once.

"There's just one more thing," said Leonard, as he tucked in to a giant slice of cake. "Could you all stay here tonight?...just to keep me company!"

Miss Mole Baby-sits

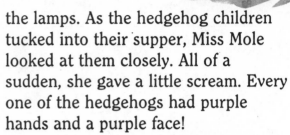

One morning Mrs Hedgehog received a letter in the mail. It was an invitation to go out to supper.

"I really would like to go," sighed Mrs Hedgehog as she read the invitation out loud, "but who will look after my ten little hedgehogs?"

Now Miss Mole, who was scurrying by to fetch her morning newspaper, overheard Mrs Hedgehog as she stood on her doorstep. "I'd love to baby-sit for you," offered Miss Mole. "I'm very fond of your ten children, and they know me very well."

So that was settled. The very next evening, at seven o'clock on the dot, Mrs Hedgehog went out to supper in her very best dress. And a very excited Miss Mole took charge of ten little hedgehogs.

"Can we go out to play in the woods for a while?" the eldest hedgehog asked Miss Mole.

"Of course you can, but remember to come back as soon as it begins to get dark."

The ten little hedgehogs were very good and as soon as the sun sank behind the hill, they came home at once.

As they came through the front door, Miss Mole counted each one. There were ten little hedgehogs all safe and sound. Miss Mole sighed with relief. "Come into the kitchen and eat your supper, but first wash your hands and faces!"

Miss Mole busied about the kitchen setting the table and lighting the lamps. As the hedgehog children tucked into their supper, Miss Mole looked at them closely. All of a sudden, she gave a little scream. Every one of the hedgehogs had purple hands and a purple face!

"We've been picking blackberries!" piped up Baby Hedgehog, "and these are for you." From under the table two of the children lifted up a huge basket of juicy blackberries.

"How very kind," said Miss Mole with a gasp, "but how on earth am I going to get you clean before your mother comes home?"

As soon as the little hedgehogs had gobbled up their supper, Miss Mole hurried them into the bathroom. But however hard she rubbed and scrubbed with soap and brushes, not one bit of purple dye came off the ten little hedgehogs.

"Oh dear!" cried Miss Mole quite worn out. "Whatever shall I do?"

"I know," laughed Baby Hedgehog, and from the bathroom cupboard he pulled a big bottle of bubble bath.

Straight away, Miss Mole turned on the taps, filled up the bath and all the little hedgehogs jumped in.

What a time they had! There were bubbles everywhere and quite a few puddles on the bathroom floor as well. After a long soak everyone was clean, and every trace of the purple had disappeared completely.

The ten little hedgehogs were tired out, so they went to bed and fell fast asleep - and so did Miss Mole!

Bobby Rabbit And Mr. Fox

Bobby Rabbit was very lazy. He hated cleaning his house. He hated washing up, but most of all he hated drawing water from the well. As he filled up the buckets, he muttered to himself, "This is too big and the water is too heavy. This is no job for a clever rabbit like me!"

Now Mr. Fox, who was hiding round the back of the house overheard Bobby Rabbit. He smiled slyly to himself, thought for a while, then came up with a cunning plan.

The very next day, when Bobby Rabbit was drawing water from the well, Mr. Fox paid him a visit.

"Good morning Bobby Rabbit!" called Mr. Fox, as he strode down the garden path carrying a cardboard box. "No more heaving buckets of water for you. I have the perfect answer to all your problems!"

Bobby Rabbit put down his buckets and rushed over to look in the fox's box.

"Taps!" cried Bobby holding up two shiny, silver taps. "Why didn't I think of that?"

So straight away he paid Mr. Fox all the money in his money box and thanked him for his trouble.

"I shall never have to fill another bucket as long as I live!" chuckled Bobby, as he nailed the two taps to the wall above his kitchen sink. "I'll boil the kettle and make myself a pot of tea!" He turned on the cold water tap. Nothing happened! So, he turned on the hot water tap. Still nothing happened, not one drop of water!

Bobby looked underneath, he poked his fingers into the holes, he even banged the taps with a hammer. Still nothing happened!

Aunt May, who was passing by, called in to find out what all the banging was about.

"I bought these taps and they don't work!" snapped Bobby, very cross indeed.

Aunt May laughed. "You'll have to fetch water from the well for a while longer, you silly rabbit! You must ask a plumber to connect your taps to the main water supply before any water will flow through!"

Bobby Rabbit looked upset. "I've been tricked by that sly old fox!"

"I'm afraid you have!" giggled Aunt May. "Now go and get a bucket of water from the well and we'll both have a cup of tea!"

Ogden And The Dinosaur

For the first time in his life, Ogden had a bedroom all to himself. Ogden's room had new curtains, carpet, new drawers and a wardrobe, but the thing Ogden liked best of all was his new bed cover.

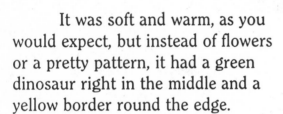

It was soft and warm, as you would expect, but instead of flowers or a pretty pattern, it had a green dinosaur right in the middle and a yellow border round the edge.

"What a great cover!" said Ogden, as he threw himself down on the bed.

"Watch where you're putting your elbows!" said a voice.

Before Ogden could reply, there was a green dinosaur standing on his new carpet, and the bed cover was quite empty - except for the yellow border round the edge!

"What are our plans for today?" the dinosaur asked Ogden eagerly.

"You're a dinosaur!" gasped Ogden, with his mouth wide open. "I have a green dinosaur in my new bedroom!"

The dinosaur pushed open the bedroom door. "Jump up and we'll go for a ride!"

Ogden rode his green dinosaur down the drive, out of the gate and down the lane. They went on through the wood, up the hill, stopped a while at the top, then back down again.

"What do you eat?" Ogden asked his new friend. "Not people, I hope!"

"No, I prefer green things, like apples and cress, and I love sprouting broccoli and kale!" said the dinosaur.

"Would a cauliflower do?" Ogden asked as they rode past a vegetable stall.

"A boxful would be nice," said the dinosaur licking his lips, "and a few lettuce to finish with!"

Ogden rode back on his dinosaur and waved to everyone he knew. "A green dinosaur! How exciting!" they all said.

When they went upstairs, Ogden threw himself on the bed. He stared at the bed cover and there was the green dinosaur back in the middle. But Ogden was sure he heard a voice say, "See you tomorrow!"

Mildred Moves House

Mildred the country mouse thought it was about time she moved house. "It's getting far too busy near this road and sometimes it can be quite dangerous!" she told her children. "My cousin has sent word that there is a fallen tree to rent near her," she went on, "it's in a quiet lane and sounds like a perfect place for our new home!"

The four little mice could hardly wait to pack up and move on, for they had always wanted to live in a tree, full of secret passages and hiding places.

Mildred's neighbours made her and her family feel very welcome. They brought baskets full of tasty treats to eat, honey flavoured drinks and a chocolate drop or two for each of the children.

"Is there anything at all you need for your new home?" Mildred's cousin asked kindly.

"Indeed there is," Mildred replied. "I would like some nutshells!"

Now wasn't that a strange request!

Nevertheless, two of the strongest mice fetched a bag full of nutshells and emptied them out on the floor in front of Mildred.

"Oh my goodness!" she cried. "These are no good, they're broken into little pieces!"

What Mildred really needed was a few large empty nutshells...and this is what she made with them...

The Grumpy Teddy Bears

People came every day to look in the window, but no-one came inside the shop to buy. Grandpa Button felt very disappointed.

Along a certain street in Toy Village is a very special shop which sells all kinds of teddy bears. Children come from far and wide to choose the bears and take them home to love them forever.

But it wasn't always so! Many years ago, Grandpa Button spent all day long making teddies, but he never sold a single one.

His shop window was always full of bears in all colours and sizes. There were honey coloured bears with black stitched noses, golden teddies with soft suede paws, white bears, black bears and cuddly brown ones that growled when you gave them a squeeze.

Then one day, Grandpa Button's cousin Emily paid a visit to Toy Village. As she passed the shop window, she looked at all the teddies and gave a little scream.

Grandpa Button put down his work and rushed outside.

"Look at all the teddies' faces!" cried cousin Emily, pointing at the window. "You've stitched their smiles on upside down. No wonder no-one buys the poor things, they all look so grumpy!" Grandpa Button had to agree.

"We can soon change all that," said cousin Emily, as she came inside and took off her coat. Straight away, she pulled out her sewing kit, and with her needle and thread she soon stitched happy smiles onto every teddy bear.

It wasn't very long before all the teddy bears in the window were sold. Cousin Emily couldn't refuse staying with Grandpa Button and helping him make hundreds more teddies for children everywhere to love!

Fizzy Grizzly

Fizzy Grizzly lived in a forest park. He was a very friendly grizzly bear and liked to wander along the paths and tracks to meet the hikers and backpackers, and talk to the folks camping and walking in the forest.

Sometimes he would give them quite a shock as he popped out from behind the trees, but Fizzy Grizzly would shake hands and offer to show them the way. He would even help to put up their tents and build camp fires.

Soon the visitors got to know Fizzy. He made lots of new friends and went to picnics and barbecues every single day!

Now perhaps you may be wondering how a grizzly bear got such a strange name!

Visitors to the park called him Fizzy because he loved fizzy drinks! In cans, or bottles, or from a glass with a straw - Fizzy loved them all!

He drank so many fizzy drinks, he often had the hiccups. You could hear Fizzy all over the park. Hic! Hic! Hic! All day long!

In the evening, Fizzy would sit round the campers' fires and drink a whole boxful of fizzy drinks. Then he would hiccup all the way home through the forest in the moonlight, waking up the other animals as he passed by. Hic! Hic! Hic!

Now when the first few flakes of snow began to fall in the park, it meant that winter was on the way. Then Fizzy Grizzly would say goodbye to his friends and go home to hibernate until spring.

Fizzy Grizzly enjoyed his long winter sleep, snug and warm in his bed, when the world outside was frozen and cold. But sad to say, no-one else did!

Fizzy Grizzly had been drinking fizzy drinks all summer long, so he hiccuped loudly until he woke up in the spring.

Hic! Hic! Hic! Fizzy Grizzly slept peacefully. Hic! Hic! Hic! Everyone else was wide awake!

The Bad-tempered Spinning Top

Once upon a time there was a brightly coloured spinning top. He lived with the rest of the toys on a little girl's bedroom floor.

Now the spinning top was a bad-tempered fellow, he liked his own way and could be quite horrid at times. Some days when he was in a bad mood, he would whizz round and round the bedroom floor spinning on the toys' toes, or pushing them hard against the wall.

"Get out of the way, you stupid things!" he hummed, as he flew round the room. "I need more space than you!"

The toys got out of the way as fast as they could, for a top on your toes can be quite painful.

Now one day, the top made up his mind to take a look at the world outside, so he spun out of the house and down the street without even saying goodbye.

As the top whirled along, he spotted a large playground. "What a perfect place for me to spin!" cried the top, and with that he shot through the gate and began to whizz round and round.

All of a sudden, something hit the top and he went hurtling across the playground. He only just managed to stay upright and keep spinning!

Then without any warning, something else crashed into him. The poor top flew up into the air and landed upside down, still spinning! Then he felt another bang and another. Bang! Crash! Wallop! He stopped spinning at once and took a look around.

There in the playground were four boys practising on skateboards. The top had been far too busy whirling round to notice them. The boys were having a wonderful time on their skateboards and they didn't see the top at all!

"Now I know what the toys feel like when I spin on their toes," said the top rather sadly.

He went back home and said he was very sorry to the toys...and sometimes, but only if he is asked, the top will give a special spinning display to tunes played by the toy music box!

Ready Teddy's Big Adventure

When Teddy was invited to parties he would choose an extra special costume. It took him simply ages to get dressed, and when his friends came to call they would shout, "Are you ready Teddy?" But Teddy never was, so his friends called him 'Ready Teddy'!

Once upon a time, there was a Teddy Bear who loved to dress up. In the street where he lived was a costume shop, so Teddy could borrow a different set of clothes every day.

Sometimes he would be a cowboy or an indian chief, another day he would dress as a pirate or a wizard.

Once when Ready Teddy was dressed as a racing driver, he was asked to take part in a race. Then to Ready Teddy's great surprise, he came in first and won the prize!

"Why do you like dressing up so much?" his friends asked him.

"Because sometimes, I have an adventure!" laughed the bear.

But even Ready Teddy could not have dreamed of the adventure he would have the day he put on a space suit!

"I've always wanted to be an astronaut," said Ready Teddy as he admired himself in the mirror of the costume shop. "I would love to go to the moon!"

As Ready Teddy walked along the street, a taxi pulled up alongside him.

"Can I take you to the launching pad?" said the driver, so Ready Teddy jumped inside.

When the taxi stopped, he could hardly believe his eyes, for there, waiting to be launched, was an enormous silver rocket.

"I think I'll take a look inside," said Ready Teddy, climbing up the launching ramp.

The door at the very top of the rocket was open, and that is where Ready Teddy's adventure began.

Before he knew what was happening, the rocket was launched on it's journey through space with Ready Teddy at the controls.

At last it landed on the moon and Ready Teddy, in his astronaut's suit, got out, took a look around, then went for a ride in a moon buggy.

"I'd better hoist a flag, just to show I've been here!" said Ready Teddy proudly. And after that, he took a last look around and got back into his rocket.

At the end of a long journey, Ready Teddy splashed down safely in the sea. A boat picked him up and took him to shore where the taxi was waiting.

"Take me back to the costume shop please!" Ready Teddy told the taxi driver.

"I'm going to choose another costume, and maybe I shall have another adventure as exciting as this one!"

Woolly Rabbit Gets Wet

One summer night, Woolly Rabbit was left outside in the garden. He was rather small, so when the children collected up their toys, they must have missed him.

That night, it rained and rained. The rag doll, who was very fond of the rabbit, was so worried, she almost cried!

The next day the children's puppy found Woolly Rabbit under a bush. His fur was wet and soggy and he looked very sorry for himself.

The children squeezed the water out of their rabbit, then hung him on the washing line to dry. Woolly Rabbit didn't like that one bit!

At last, he was fluffy and dry and put back with the other toys. The rag doll was overjoyed to see him return safe and sound.

"This must never happen again!" she said hugging Woolly Rabbit very tightly.

So she found a red ribbon from the sewing box and tied it in a big bow around the rabbit's neck. On the end of the ribbon, she sewed a little silver bell left over from Christmas.

"Now you'll never get left outside again!" she smiled, and gave Woolly Rabbit a great big hug!

Ten Noisy Little Hedgehogs

When all the ten little hedgehogs were at school, Mrs Hedgehog would often remark how peaceful and quiet the house was! But when they returned at four o'clock, it could get a little noisy!

One day, when the hedgehogs came home they were very excited. As they ran through the door, each one was carrying a musical instrument.

"We are learning to play tunes together," said the eldest. "Let's play you one now!"

So Mrs Hedgehog sat down in her chair to listen.

The ten little hedgehogs stood in a group, opened their music books, took a deep breath and began to play.

"Oh my goodness," gasped Mrs Hedgehog as she sat up in her chair, "what a dreadful noise!"

The ten little hedgehogs played on and on and the music got worse and worse. At last they stopped and Baby Hedgehog climbed up onto his mother's knee. "I think we need to practise!" he said with a grin.

Night after night, the little hedgehogs played their music together, but however hard they practised, they never sounded any better. Poor Mrs Hedgehog got no peace at all!

Now one morning, while the little hedgehogs were at school, Mrs Hedgehog sat quietly reading a magazine. Suddenly, she spied an advertisement on the very last page. When she read it, she jumped up from her chair with glee, for this was the very thing she had been looking for!

A few days later the postman delivered a long flat box to Mrs Hedgehog and when the children came home at four o'clock, they found a surprise waiting for them.

It was a xylophone! The notes sounded soft and melodic, and everyone could play together - even Baby Hedgehog!

Soon the children were playing beautiful tunes and all their woodland neighbours came regularly to listen.

Edward The Flying Elephant

Do you believe that elephants can fly? Edward can! He flies high in the sky above the clouds then dives down low, almost touching the ground. Sometimes he loops the loop or flies upside down, which gives his passengers a fright!

One day, while Edward was checking his plane, he heard a message on his radio:

Two explorers are missing in the Great Rainforest. Can anyone help?

Straight away, Edward jumped into his plane and took off. "I'll fly over the Great Rainforest and see if I can find them before it gets dark!"

It didn't take Edward long to spot the two explorers as he dived down low over the trees. They were paddling their canoe down the river which wound through the dense forest.

"No wonder they're lost," said Edward out loud. "They're going the wrong way! There's nowhere for me to land, so how can I tell them to head back?"

All of a sudden, Edward had a brilliant idea! Quickly he turned his plane round and flew high up into the sky. He looped the loop a couple of times then made a directing arrow with smoke from his plane.

The two explorers saw it straight away and understood what it meant. They turned their canoe round and in next to no time had paddled back up the river and returned safe and sound.

Wasn't it lucky for them that elephants really can fly!

Yellow Feather Goes Hunting

Once upon a time, there was a little Indian boy called Yellow Feather. He lived at the bottom of a wide canyon.

One day, his father gave him his very own bow and lots of tiny arrows. Little Yellow Feather felt very proud, and every night, he dreamed he was a great hunter.

"Hear me, all you creatures!" shouted Yellow Feather. "Flee for your lives, for here comes the greatest hunter in the whole valley!" The little Indian's voice echoed round the rocks as he ran through the hot, dusty canyon.

All of a sudden, Yellow Feather spied a lizard lying by a rock. "Go away little boy and don't point that arrow at me!" yawned the lizard and went back to sleep in the hot sun.

Next Yellow Feather spotted an armadillo scurrying across the path. He took aim straight away!

"Stop playing games with that bow and arrow. It's far too hot!" said the armadillo and with that he rolled himself into a ball and went to sleep too!

Then all of a sudden, a roadrunner sped by and Yellow Feather ran after him as fast as he could.

With the speed of lightning, the roadrunner ran through the canyon and into the desert. Then he ran round and round the cactus until he made little Yellow Feather feel quite dizzy.

"Can't catch me with your bow and arrow!" squealed the roadrunner. Then he disappeared in cloud of dust.

Little Yellow Feather sat on the ground. "I'm lost and a long way from home," he said, trying hard not to cry. "Whatever shall I do?"

Just then, a friendly coyote came by. He could see that Yellow Feather was alone and needed someone to help him.

So the coyote scrambled up onto a flat rock, sat down and lifted back his head and gave his wildest coyote howl. The sound could be heard right to the edge of the wide canyon. Then another coyote took up the howl, then another and another, all the way down the canyon until Yellow Feather's father heard the call.

At once, he understood what was wrong. He jumped on his fastest horse and galloped off to find little Yellow Feather.

The coyote's calls guided him far into the canyon, where he found his son sitting by the side of his new friend the coyote...who was still howling!

The Runaway Toys

Once upon a time, there was an old toy maker who made clockwork toys. People came from near and far to buy them and to watch them all whirring around in his tiny shop.

Sometimes, the toy maker made clockwork mice that darted all over the floor. Sometimes, he made birds that hopped across the table. He even made a set of false teeth that rattled and snapped as they span round and round!

The clockwork toys worked so well, they would whizz all over the place. But some got lost behind cupboards and others walked off the window ledge onto the roof below, where the old toy maker couldn't reach them.

One day, a visitor to the shop solved the problem. Out of his coat pocket he pulled a huge magnet. He tied one end of a piece of string to a long stick and the other round the magnet.

Soon he was collecting up all the lost toys that were out of reach. The old man was delighted and spent all that day playing with the runaway toys!

Lucy's Lunch

It was almost lunch-time and Lucy the long-legged goose was feeling rather hungry. "I wish the farmer's wife would hurry up and feed us!" said Lucy impatiently. "I think I will go and find out where she is!"

So straight away Lucy dashed over to the farmhouse and peeped through the window. Inside was the farmer's wife making lunch for the farmer.

As Lucy the goose looked into the kitchen she could hardly believe her eyes. "My favourite!" smiled Lucy. "Lots and lots of big fat juicy long wriggling worms!"

And with that she ran back to the farmyard to tell the others what a treat was in store for them at lunch-time.

At last, the farmer's wife opened her kitchen door and scattered handfuls of corn into the farmyard as usual.

"Where are all those lovely juicy worms I saw you cooking on the kitchen stove earlier?" cried Lucy.

Just then the farmer came round the corner. "That's my favourite lunch Lucy!" he said with a grin. "Spaghetti in tomato sauce - not worms!"

Everybody in the farmyard fell about laughing. That was, excepting Lucy the long-legged goose, who felt rather silly!

The Mischievous Fox Cub

Rusty the fox cub was always up to mischief. Whenever he went out to play, his mother would say, "Rusty, try not to get into any mischief and don't poke your nose into other people's business!" But Rusty did - all the time! He just couldn't help himself!

One day, the mischievous little fox cub went to take a look at Mrs Swan sitting on her eggs by the river bank. Now swans can be fierce, but Rusty didn't know that and almost lost his tail!

Another time when he was passing the farmyard gate, he decided to pop inside, just to find out where Mr Turkey lived. Now Rusty didn't know that turkeys do not like foxes, not even little ones. This time Rusty got a sharp peck on the nose - and he was only trying to be friendly!

"Oh dear!" said Rusty to himself, as he trotted through the wood. "I really must try not to get into any more mischief!"

Just then, he heard a rustling in the undergrowth. "I'll just find out what made that noise," he said, sticking his nose into a pile of dry leaves.

"Ouch!" Rusty yelped, as he jumped back. Something had pricked him right on the nose and it really hurt.

"Sorry!" said a tiny voice. Then out from under the leaves came a little hedgehog. "Didn't your mother ever tell you not to poke your nose into other people's business?" giggled the prickly little hedgehog. Rusty had to laugh too!

173

Snowy The Seagull

Snowy the seagull loved the lifeboat. Everyday he would watch from the cliff top, just in case it was launched into the sea below. "I don't think I shall be lucky today," said Snowy with a sigh. "The sea is so calm and still, nobody will need the lifeboat!"

So, he flew off to join the other gulls on top of the rocks...but the gulls were not alone, sitting on top of the rocks were three children looking very frightened.

"We came to take photographs of the gulls and our boat has floated away!" said one of them.

"The water is rising very fast," said another. "What shall we do?"

"Don't worry!" called Snowy, as he flew away. "I'll bring help!" Then the seagull flew across the water straight to the lifeboat station.

At once, the crew launched the lifeboat. "Fly above us," called the Captain to Snowy, "and show us the way to the rocks as fast as you can."

All of a sudden, a strong wind began to blow and storm clouds gathered. The lifeboat started to toss about in the huge waves.

"Can you see those rocks?" the Captain shouted to Snowy above the noise of the gale.

Just at that moment the seagull saw the children. Now there was only one tiny piece of rock left for them to cling to. Snowy flew down and landed beside them. "Hang on!" said the gull. "Help is on the way!"

At last, the lifeboat came into view and the crew rescued the children. Soon they were all back at the lifeboat station, safe and dry.

"You're quite a hero. Snowy!" laughed the Captain. "I think you ought to join our crew, then you could keep a look out for anyone in trouble on the rocks. Well done, Snowy, look out for the lifeboat!"

The Turtle's Slippery Slide

One winter's day, it was frosty and cold and everywhere was white with snow. It was a perfect day for climbing up the nearest hill and sliding down to the bottom.

Everyone was searching their garages and looking in lofts for sledges and toboggans.

"Race you up to the top of the hill!" yelled one of the bears, who was carrying an old tin bath.

"Race you down to the bottom!" shouted another, perched on a big wooden tray.

Then everybody slid down the hill all at once. Two on a toboggan, three sharing a sledge, all skimming and sliding down the slippery slope to land in soft piles of snow at the bottom.

It was such wonderful fun whizzing down the hill and trudging back up again, especially for the little green turtle. He didn't need a toboggan, or a sledge, or a tin bath, or a tray. In fact, he didn't need anything at all!

The Flying Display

Gerry the pilot felt very proud. He had been chosen to be the leader in the flying display at the air show in one weeks time.

"Wonderful!" exclaimed Gerry, and rushed across the airfield to tell the other pilots. Now because he was so excited, or perhaps he just didn't look where he was going, Gerry tripped, fell flat on his face and sprained his ankle!

"Sorry," said the doctor, who looked at Gerry's leg. "No more flying for two whole weeks!"

Poor Gerry, he looked so disappointed.

On the afternoon of the flying display, Gerry sat outside the control tower looking very glum indeed.

Although he couldn't take part, his pilot friends made sure that he cheered up and enjoyed the show!

The Twins Keep Busy

Aunt Janet had asked the twins to come and stay with her lots of times, but Meg and Martin always had an excuse.

"We really don't want to go!" the twins told their mother. "There's nothing to do at Aunt Janet's and it will be very boring!"

"Go and stay for just one night," said Mother with a little smile. "You may be surprised!"

So one weekend, when Meg and Martin couldn't think of any more excuses, they went off to Aunt Janet's for the night.

"I'm afraid I haven't any toys for you to play with," said their aunt, as she opened the door to the twins. "But there's plenty to keep you amused in the kitchen!"

"I hope she doesn't want us to cook or wash up!" Martin whispered.

"Sssh," replied Meg, as she stepped inside. "She'll hear you!"

Aunt Janet's kitchen was huge with a large pine table full of all kinds of things.

"Hey!" cried Martin as he sat down. "Face paints and glue. Look, there's plaster and clay, there's even papier maché!"

"Make as much mess as you like," Aunt Janet laughed. "I'll join you and make a mess too!"

The twins soon found that Aunt Janet was brilliant at making models and kites, all kinds of costumes and very scary masks.

She could make paper dolls that stretched across the room, and trees from rolled up newspaper that almost reached the ceiling.

The hours passed so quickly it was soon time for bed.

"Don't bother clearing up the mess," called Aunt Janet as she made the supper. "We'll make a lot more tomorrow!"

Next morning they had breakfast in a tree house that Aunt Janet had put up a few years ago. By lunch-time, they knew how to make stilts from tin cans, read a compass and build a puppet theatre from a cardboard box.

Aunt Janet showed them how to cook quick home-made pizzas with frothy milkshakes, and chocolate crunchies for lunch.

Would you believe that the twins stayed with Aunt Janet a whole week, there was so much to do!

When they went home at last, it took ages to tell their mother about all the things they had done.

"I know!" she said with a grin. "I did exactly the same when we used to play together as children!"

Ogden's Rainy Day

Ogden had a new bed cover with a green dinosaur design right in the middle. Whenever he closed his eyes tight and threw himself down on the cover, there was a green dinosaur standing on his new bedroom carpet!

"What are we going to do today?" the dinosaur asked Ogden as he trundled across to the window.

"Look outside," Ogden sighed. "It's pouring with rain, so we shall have to stay indoors."

"Not a bit of it!" snorted the dinosaur. "I've never been outside in the rain before, so let's get moving!"

"You'll get very wet!" grinned Ogden, pulling on his coat and boots.

"Never mind," giggled the dinosaur. "I'm waterproof!"

Once the green dinosaur was outside, the fun began. His enormous feet splashed through the puddles and wet Ogden and his friends from top to toe. His giant tail swished from side to side spraying water over everyone.

"Isn't rain wonderful!" shouted the dinosaur.

"It is if you're waterproof!" Ogden yelled back, dripping wet.

The green dinosaur was enjoying himself so much that he forgot where he was putting his big feet. He travelled over the wet grass, on through the flower beds and was soon covered in thick sticky mud. When he swished his tail from left to right, mud flew everywhere, and this made matters even worse.

"How are we going to get you clean?" gasped poor Ogden. "I've never seen so much mud!"

"Don't worry," laughed the dinosaur. "I think it looks good!"

But Ogden was thinking about his new bedroom carpet when they got back to the house.

As Ogden and his friends hurried home in the rain with a very dirty dinosaur, they passed a garage.

In one corner of the forecourt was just the thing they needed - a car wash!

Ogden pressed a coin into the machine and very soon the dinosaur was clean and sparkling once more.

"Did you enjoy going out in the rain?" Ogden asked the green dinosaur when they got back to his bedroom. But as Ogden threw himself onto the bed, he stared at the bed cover - and there was the green dinosaur back in the middle once again!

Tim's New Soap

Tim loved playing with water, but he hated getting washed! He hated washing behind his ears and the back of his neck, but most of all he hated washing his face.

The rest of Tim's family loved getting washed and spent hours in the bathroom. Tim found this very strange indeed!

Now one day, when Tim was out shopping, he bought some trick soap from the joke shop. Tim read the label, *Guaranteed to turn your hands and face red when you get washed!* What fun he would have with that!

"I'll leave it on the wash basin," sniggered Tim, "and wait to see what happens!"

Mother used the bathroom first, but she had a shower and used her own shower gel.

Sister Sue took hours in the bathroom, but she used the perfumed soap her boyfriend had given her. Tim could smell it all over the house.

No-one used the trick soap at all and Tim went off to bed that night rather disappointed.

Next morning, Tim overslept. "Hurry up!" called Mother up the stairs. "Get washed and dressed as quickly as you can, or you will miss the school bus."

Tim jumped out of bed, grabbed his clothes and ran into the bathroom. He filled the basin with hot water, reached for the soap and washed himself at double speed. Quickly, he ran downstairs getting dressed as he went.

"You've just time for some breakfast!" called his mother from the kitchen.

But dear oh dear, as Tim sat down at the kitchen table, the whole family burst out laughing.

"What have you done to your face and hands?" asked Father, laughing so much he almost choked on his toast!

"Look in the mirror!" Sue shrieked, pointing at him.

Tim looked at himself and then he remembered. He had picked up the trick soap by mistake, his face was all red and so were his hands. The joke was on him!

The trick soap took ages to wash off. Tim was late for school and had to explain to his teacher - and she laughed loudest of all!

Take Me For A Ride

Robin liked cars. He had a box full of model cars that he played with everyday. He loved trips out in his father's car and never got bored however long the journey.

"I wish I could drive a car," said Robin to his father one day as they were driving along.

"I'm afraid you'll have to wait a long time before you can learn," his father laughed. "In the mean time, you'll have to be a passenger!"

Now on his next birthday, Robin was given a pedal car as a present. He thought it was wonderful and drove it everyday.

"How do you like driving?" joked his father, as the little boy raced up and down the path in his new car.

"It's great," Robin replied, "but I wish I had a passenger to ride around with me."

"I don't think your car is quite big enough," laughed Daddy. "You'll have to wait a few years until you can drive a real car, then you'll have plenty of passengers."

But Robin didn't have to wait *that* long. He looked outside and found a passenger waiting to be taken for a ride straight away!

The Great Green Caterpillar

One warm afternoon, a tiny brown sparrow was splashing around in the birdbath in the middle of the lawn. All of a sudden, he glanced down and saw the biggest caterpillar you can ever imagine moving along the garden path.

Straight away, he flew up into the apple tree and told the magpie. "It's almost as long as a snake!" chirped the tiny sparrow, "with lots and lots of bright green legs!"

The magpie flapped his wings. "I love caterpillars, especially big and juicy bright green ones. I shall have it for my tea!"

Now the woodpecker on the branch above heard him and said, "That enormous caterpillar will be far too big for you. I shall fly down and help you gobble it up!"

So, the birds flew out of the tree and landed right next to the giant caterpillar.

"Nobody is going to eat us!" croaked lots of little voices that seemed to be coming from the caterpillar.

The startled magpie and the woodpecker fell over backwards with fright.

You see the giant caterpillar was made up of lots and lots of green frogs. "This costume for the lakeside party this afternoon certainly fooled you two greedy birds!" giggled the cheeky frogs.

Creepy Crawler

There was once a gigantic tractor that ran on tracks, not wheels. Now this tractor was very strong, but very, very slow. He crawled along, moving heavy logs through the forest, no faster than a snail. So that is why the lumberjacks called him Creepy Crawler!

Moving the trunks of great pine trees was very hard work. As soon as the lumberjacks had cut them down, Creepy Crawler and his driver would carefully drag the logs to the sawmill to be cut into pieces.

Creepy Crawler and his driver worked all day long and in all kinds of weather.

"You're the strongest tractor in the whole forest!" the driver told Creepy Crawler as they drove through the tall pine trees. "That is why you have been chosen to do a very special job today!"

"How exciting," said Creepy Crawler. "I shall do my very best!"

When they reached the middle of the forest, the lumberjacks were busy cutting down the biggest pine tree of all, it's branches almost reached the sky.

At last, it toppled to the ground, just missing Creepy Crawler's bonnet!

Very carefully, the men harnessed the great tree to the back of the gigantic tractor, and very slowly they moved off.

After what seemed ages, they left the forest behind. They travelled slowly past the sawmill and went on into town.

As Creepy Crawler moved steadily through the streets, crowds of people stood cheering and waving.

"What's all this about?" Creepy Crawler shouted to the driver.

"Haven't you guessed?" the driver laughed. "The town is going to put up the biggest Christmas tree in the world right in the middle of the square, and you have brought it safely from the forest!"

Creepy Crawler felt very proud. In fact he blushed!

"There would be no Christmas tree without you!" shouted the crowd. They covered Creepy Crawler with trimmings, streamers and a long string of sparkling Christmas lights!